P9-BJY-004

The First
Husband

Also by Laura Dave

....

The Divorce Party

London Is the Best City in America

The First Husband

Laura Dave

VIKING

VIKING
Published by the Penguin Group
Penguin Group (USA) Inc., 375 Hudson Street,
New York, New York 10014, U.S.A.
Penguin Group (Canada), 90 Eglinton Avenue East, Suite 700,
Toronto, Ontario, Canada M4P2Y3
(a division of Pearson Penguin Canada Inc.)
Penguin Books Ltd, 80 Strand, London WC2R 0RL, England
Penguin Ireland, 25 St. Stephen's Green, Dublin 2, Ireland
(a division of Penguin Books Ltd)
Penguin Books Australia Ltd, 250 Camberwell Road, Camberwell,
Victoria 3124, Australia
(a division of Pearson Australia Group Pty Ltd)
Penguin Books India Pvt Ltd, II Community Centre, Panchsheel Park,
New Delhi – 110 017, India
Penguin Group (NZ), 67 Apollo Drive, Rosedale, North Shore 0632,
New Zealand (a division of Pearson New Zealand Ltd)
Penguin Books (South Africa) (Pty) Ltd, 24 Sturdee Avenue,
Rosebank, Johannesburg 2196, South Africa

Penguin Books Ltd, Registered Offices:
80 Strand, London WC2R 0RL, England

First published in 2011 by Viking Penguin,
a member of Penguin Group (USA) Inc.

1   3   5   7   9   10   8   6   4   2

Copyright © Laura Dave, 2011
All rights reserved

Publisher's Note
This is a work of fiction. Names, characters, places, and incidents either are the product of the
author's imagination or are used fictitiously, and any resemblance to actual persons, living or dead,
business establishments, events, or locales is entirely coincidental.

LIBRARY OF CONGRESS CATALOGINGIN PUBLICATION DATA
Dave, Laura.
The first husband / Laura Dave.
p. cm.
ISBN 978-0-670-02267-0
1. Travel writers—Fiction.   2. Divorced people—Fiction.   3. Marriage—Fiction.
4. Massachusetts—Fiction.   5. Psychological fiction.   I. Title.
PS3604.A938F57 2011
813'.6—dc22
2010045257

Printed in the United States of America
Set in Fairfield LH
Designed by Alissa Amell

Without limiting the rights under copyright reserved above, no part of this publicaton may be
reproduced, stored in or introduced into a retrieval system, or transmitted, in any form or by any
means (electronic, mechanical, photocopying, recording or otherwise), without the prior written
permission of both the copyright owner and the above publisher of this book.

The scanning, uploading, and distribution of this book via the Internet or via any other means
without the permission of the publisher is illegal and punishable by law. Please purchase
only authorized electronic editions and do not participate in or encourage electronic piracy of
copyrightable materials. Your support of the author's rights is appreciated.

For Josh, always

Turn up the lights. I don't want to go home in the dark.

—O. HENRY

Part 1

Once Upon a Time . . .

It feels important to start with the truth about how I got here. When everything gets messy and brutal and complicated, the truth is the first thing to go, isn't it? People try to shade it or spin it or fix it. As though fixing the facts will make the situation less messy and brutal and complicated. Not more. But there's no fixing this. The truth is that I brought it on myself. All of it. Everything that was coming next—everything I couldn't have begun to imagine would constitute the next year of my life. After all, I was the one who did it that morning, knowing full well what could happen, what history had taught me would happen, if I were reckless enough to go through with it. I went down to the living room, still wearing Nick's oversized pajama top, and snuggled myself under the blanket, turning on the DVD player. Like it was that easy. Like *Roman Holiday* was just any movie. Like it wasn't a bomb I was about to detonate right into the middle of my life.

I'm not normally—not, as a rule, at least—a superstitious person. But there are hard and true facts that can't be ignored. The first time I saw *Roman Holiday*, I was seven years old and watched it during family movie night with both my parents. The following day they announced they were getting a divorce. The next time I was sixteen. My mother proclaimed later that day, post-viewing, that she was moving us—our ninth move in nine years—this time away from San Francisco (where we'd lived just long enough for me to find a real friend, a "boyfriend," and a potential other friend) to a tiny town in the northeast corner of North Dakota (population 351, where I'd attend my last year of high school with three people in my entire graduating class).

Five years later I'd just graduated from college and landed a job at the *New York Sun*. I'd be the lowliest reporter imaginable, but I'd be a reporter. In New York City! While I was packing, I came across *Roman Holiday* and thought, I'm a grown-up now, not subject to childhood superstitions. *Why not?* Here's why not: the next morning, I received an e-mail from my once-future employer. *Due to cutbacks, we have frozen all future hires. . . .* et cetera. I had less than forty-eight hours left in my college apartment, $105,000 in school loans, and the sum total of my accumulated savings sunk into a security deposit for the only apartment I could afford—a 300-square-foot studio right by the West Side Highway. And no job, not anymore.

The fourth time I was twenty-seven. Nick and I had just celebrated our one-year anniversary and were getting ready to move across the country together, to Los Angeles. Nick was trying to break into movies, a feat that demanded the move. Which was fine with me—exciting, even. I was writing a weekly travel column for a newspaper in Philadelphia and since I'd been traveling for the paper an average of two hundred days a year anyway, they were more than willing to let my new home base be Los Angeles.

And so I turned on *Roman Holiday,* feeling solid in my job, solid in my relationship, solid in my decision to go west, feeling there was little that the movie could mess with—a part of me, maybe, even wanting to *prove* to myself there was little it could mess with.

But halfway through (the bad didn't even wait until the end that time) the telephone rang. The house we were supposed to move into in Venice—the house where we'd already shipped 80 percent of our belongings—had burned *down*. No one seemed to know the cause. I knew the cause.

And yet there I was, four years later, thirty-two days shy of my thirty-second birthday, and what was I doing? At some point don't you get Pavlovian about it? The movie had hurt me enough times, or, at the very least, I had several of the most uncomfortable experiences of my life in bizarrely close proximity to watching it—how could I not associate it with that pain? Why would I watch it again? Here's why: I *loved* the movie. What *When Harry Met Sally* was to some of my girlfriends—or *Field of Dreams* was to Nick—*Roman Holiday* was to me.

It was my comfort movie. It was, quite simply, my comfort. Yes, my mother had admitted that she'd named me in part after Audrey Hepburn's Princess Ann. How could any young girl watch that movie without wanting to be Audrey Hepburn? But it was much more than that. Part of it might be that I was a reporter myself, a travel writer—my column, "Checking Out," was meant to provide a guide for how best to explore the most exotic and interesting places in the world. A complete guide to enjoying exciting cities/special towns/tiny islands-in-the-middle-of-the-Indian-Ocean that might be hard to navigate otherwise. Not surprisingly, I'd devoted my first column to Rome. Truthfully, it was as much an ode to *Roman Holiday*—to the experience of watching Princess Ann and reporter Joe Bradley (Gregory Peck) explore the Eternal City and escape their real lives. That's what I loved about my job—being able to explore the world, to constantly escape. But somewhere deep inside, I'd always wondered if, like Audrey's Princess Ann, I wasn't just hoping that if I fell asleep on a park bench in one of the hundreds of cities I visited, I'd wake up and get to spend a day living the exact life I always dreamed of.

The other reason I loved the movie had to do with the quality of the romance between Bradley and Ann—its incandescent charm, the happiness beneath its every beat. It led me to convince myself, as a logical person, that my tragedies couldn't possibly have anything to do with a movie that was so romantic, so full of hope. Or they wouldn't. Not this time.

So there I was, at a not-this-time moment again: thirty-one, complacent, sleepy. My brilliant and beautiful dog, Amelia (named after the original fantastic traveler and explorer, Amelia Earhart; we called her Mila, for short) and I had the morning to ourselves. Nick was working. He was a movie director, currently shooting his second movie—a thriller about vampires taking over Washington, D.C. Since his first film, a road trip movie (*not* a vampire anywhere to be seen), had been well received at a film festival where it was apparently important to be well received, he was experiencing his first taste of fame. I was so excited for him—for us, really. I had been there during the salad days, when we were shooting his short films on the street. Me as both key grip and leading lady. His sister as producer. Our dog, Mila, as . . . Dog Mila.

And yet, since his newfound success, Nick had become slightly exhausting in the way he talked about his work. For starters, he was calling it "my work." It was a phase, I knew. It was just one that I was hoping would end soon. Plus, I'd just gotten back from my own tough month on the road—spending August traveling through three separate countries (Mexico, the Dominican Republic, Argentina), working on pieces for "Checking Out." And so I decided to go for it. To treat myself. Sweet Mila laying on my lap, I pushed a button, the DVD player powered on, and I hit PLAY.

Then it came across the screen: the crisp white credits, the orchestra keying up, Rome's most famous sites in the background. The Vatican. The Wedding Cake. The ancient ruins. Until the words *News Flash* come across the screen, and there she was before us: the stunning Audrey Hepburn sitting in her carriage, waving at her minions, the saddest princess in the world.

When *The End* came and the final credit crossed the screen, I looked around our house, the one I'd been sharing with Nick since we moved to L.A.—the house we found after the other house had burned down. No vase or photograph had come tumbling to the floor. No spontaneous toaster malfunction. And the fresh tulips, the ones I'd bought at the farmers market over on Arizona for $3.99, didn't immediately die. They stayed in their almost-dead-but-still-standing position.

I rubbed the back of Mila's head. She looked up at me and lovingly met my eyes.

"I guess we're good," I said.

Then the key turned in the lock.

Nick kicked open the door, balancing his thermos, the *Los Angeles Times*, his phone. He looked closer to sixteen than thirty-six standing there in his backward baseball hat and one of the button-down shirts he lived in. All of which is to say that Nick looked like Nick, the exhausted version: a four-day scruff of beard, dark circling his eyes.

He pointed to the phone so I'd know he was on a call. Then he made a circle motion with his index finger—that motion you make when you want the person on the other end of the line to finish up already. And, whoever the other person was, he must have taken the hint, because, less then a minute later, Nick clicked shut his phone and headed toward me, dropping all of his stuff on the recliner in a messy heap.

"Hey there, stranger . . ." Nick said, leaning down to give me a kiss hello—his palm cupping the back of my head, holding me there.

"Hey back at you," I said, staying close to him for an extra beat. We were used to having long periods apart, but between my column and his movie shoot, it had been a particularly brutal time. His smell, his sweetness, felt more like the exception in my life than the reality.

As Nick got down on his knees and rubbed Mila's furry ribs—his usual *Hey honey, I'm home* greeting to her—he whispered into her ear.

"Hi, baby girl . . ." he said.

Then he took a seat next to me on the couch, stretching his arms behind his head. This close, Nick looked even more beat: his eyes red and watery from the long shoot, and from the contact lenses he'd recently begun to wear in place of the reliable wire-rimmed glasses he'd had as long as I'd known him.

I decided against giving him grief for the lenses, decided, also, against telling him about the phone call from our travel agent. We were supposed to go to London in December. I had rented a tiny house in Battersea that we could actually afford to live in while Nick worked on a project there. I could barely wait and already found myself dreaming of having an extended period of time to visit my favorite parts of one of my favorite cities: going to the theater and hiding out in ancient flea markets, spending too much time in bookshops and no time at all walking near the Tower of London. The agent had called requesting the balance on the house. I needed to know if shooting was still on schedule in vampire land, so that I could feel safe giving it to her. But that was going to have to wait.

"What are you watching?" he asked.

"Was watching, it's over now." I clicked the television off, like proof. "Just a movie. *Roman Holiday* . . ."

"We own that movie? I haven't seen it forever," he said. "I've always thought it was a little overrated."

I'd never told Nick about *Roman Holiday,* not the full

story—had never told anyone but my best friend, Jordan. I knew Nick would tell me I was crazy. Though I couldn't hold that against him. I'd think I was crazy too.

"How did last night turn out?" I asked instead.

He shook his head in a way that said, *let's not even go there.*

Then he proceeded to go there, telling me about a complicated electrical problem at the bookstore in Pasadena they had rented to film the movie's climatic scene. It was important that *that* went well. It hadn't.

When he was done, he cast his eyes down, almost closing them. "So," he said. "Annabelle Adams . . ."

I laughed. I couldn't help it. Nick never called me by my full name. He called me Annie—or Adams if we were arguing about something. Adams also if he was in the mood to be particularly sweet, loving. A confusing business, really, when I thought too much about it: Adams coming up only at our best and worst moments.

"Yes, *Nicholas Campbell* . . ." I said, jokingly.

Then I reached over and touched the side of his face. He leaned into it, catching my hand there, between his cheek and his shoulder.

"I need to talk to you about something," he said. "I've needed to talk to you about it, but you've been away and I haven't been sure exactly how . . ."

"Okay . . ."

While I'd been in Punta Cana the week before, I'd seen a couples therapist on a local morning show explain how it was aggressive behavior for a woman to look right at her husband or boyfriend when he was trying to talk about something important—that it made men think of war instead of love. Weird tip. But there I was, following the advice the best I could anyway: pulling my knees under my large top and averting my gaze, just as instructed. At least I wasn't looking right at him when he continued to speak.

"The thing is," he said, "my therapist says we may need a break."

"A break from what?" I said.

This was what I said. Like an utter and complete moron. *A break from what*—what did I think? But this was how incredibly far-fetched the idea of us taking a break from each other was to me, at that moment.

"She says I need to be on my own for a while," he said. "Without you."

I turned to look at him. There are words you can never take back. Had I just heard them? Five years. We had been together for five years. Weren't there different rules for saying them after so long? Didn't everyone have to be fully dressed?

"Why?" I asked.

"She says that I love you," he said, "but also that I'm trying to love you. That I have to stop putting everyone else first."

I watched Mila's face. *Am I missing something?* I asked her silently.

She looked back at me: *I think I want a nap.*

Meanwhile, Nick was still talking, but it was like someone dropped a ball in my throat. And I couldn't swallow it and listen at the same time. Instead, I looked around our home—the one I had designed, furnished, did 95 percent of the work to keep up. I wasn't very good at making a home, maybe. Okay: definitely, maybe. I wasn't home enough to be good at it (as evidenced by my suitcase still packed and ready by the front door). But regardless, if Nick was naming that as the game, hadn't I been the one who'd always done most of the first-putting?

"She says I need to figure out what I need for me."

She says. He kept saying that. *She says.* Three hundred times now, if I was counting correctly. Probably because he knew that if he took the *she says* out, his words sounded harsher. This was my first clear thought. My second was sadder. What had I done to make him want to leave?

Which was when he started to get to the truth.

"Also," he said, far more quietly. "There may be other reasons why I'm *confused*."

At least he had the courage to say that.

"There may be other reasons?" I said. "Do you want to check with your therapist first?"

He hit me with a sad look. "That isn't helpful," he said.

Maybe it wasn't helpful, but it was also not entirely uncalled for. Nick's "therapist" wasn't even a real therapist. He had never seen a therapist before in his life. But someone from his work had recommended that Nick meet with this woman, who was closer to a psychic, or a life counselor. Or, as she called herself on her silky blue business card, a FUTURES COUNSELOR. Meaning after hearing your stories, she told you what she saw in your future and then helped you get there, or helped you to avoid it. For, you know, $650 an hour.

This was when I realized what he was trying very hard not to tell me.

"Who is she?" I asked, but I already had a guess: Michelle Bryant, Nick's ex-girlfriend and college sweetheart. They had gone to Brown together, dated all four years there, and lived together for the last two of them. Then they had lived together in a picturesque carriage house in Brooklyn for two years after graduating. Michelle was a pediatric neurosurgeon at the University of California, up in San Francisco. And, because neurosurgery apparently wasn't impressive enough, she'd also become a special consultant to the FBI, in charge of studying brain patterns in children prone to violence. And did I mention she was drop-dead gorgeous? How could I blame Nick for still wanting to date her? *I* wanted to date her.

"It's Michelle?" I said, less like a question than a statement.

"No! I've told you that you have nothing to worry about in terms of her."

Nick forgot his sadness for just long enough to look pleased about this, like it proved something that he wasn't leaving me for the person I'd been insecure about—but for someone else entirely.

"Does she work on *The Unbowed?*"

The Unbowed was the title of Nick's movie. He'd taken it from a William Ernest Henley poem that we loved—one of several poems that we'd framed and lined up by the refrigerator in our kitchen. The lines read, "Under the bludgeoning of chance / My head is bloody, but unbowed." In more generous moments, I had loved that he was using it for the title. This wasn't a generous moment.

"It's nothing like that . . ." he mumbled under his breath. Then, in case I missed it, he shook his head for emphasis: *nothing at all.* "She's just a friend . . ." he said.

"Just a friend?"

He nodded. "A friend from home," he said. "I swear to you, nothing's happened yet."

He looked relieved about this part too. But I couldn't help but wonder why he thought that the fact he was leaving me for someone he hadn't slept with *yet* was going to make me feel better. I couldn't help but wonder why he thought I'd hear anything but the words he offered up accidentally. She's from home. Meaning, home was somewhere else. Meaning, not here. With me.

"I'm so sorry, Annie," he said. "But the truth is . . ."

Then he stopped himself. He stopped himself, like he didn't know whether to say it. Which was when he did.

"The truth is, you're away so much, Adams. You're always away."

"You're saying, she's only here because I'm . . . not?" I finished for him.

"I'm saying, I may be the one who's leaving. But if we're being honest, you're never here anyway. I'm not sure you even want to be."

That's when it happened. When my heart broke open, right in my chest.

Five years. We'd been together five years. We had a life together. Wasn't I supposed to be allowed to count on it? He had promised me I could—that I should—in the breath right after the breath where he explained that he wasn't sure how he felt about marriage. But we, he and I, were going to be more than married. *Post-married*, he'd called it. *What's a piece of paper?* Right then, it was something I could have held up like proof that he couldn't just decide this. Out of nowhere.

Was this the right moment to make my other point, that he traveled almost as much as I did? It didn't seem like it. It didn't seem like he would be open to hearing that—to hearing anything from me. He was too busy looking down, picking at his fingernails. He was picking at the dirt caught there, not in a way that he was avoiding me, but in a way that he was actually focused on it. Focused and exhausted.

When he looked back up at me, it was with a look that said, *Are we done?* I knew that look, of course. I knew all of his looks. It had been five years.

I gave him a look back. *Not yet, please. I need to understand this.*

Hadn't we been sitting here, right here, yesterday? We had. I had come home from the airport, exhausted, but stayed up so I could have a few minutes with Nick before he left for work. He'd made us peach French toast and I'd helped him rework the last scene of his movie. The very last shot. He had looked so happy when he figured it out, so happy with me that I had helped. He gave a huge smile and then leaned in toward me. He leaned in toward me, just yesterday, and said, *You're priceless . . . You know that?*

It was a moment, less than twenty-four lousy hours before, which seemed directly antithetical to this moment. I didn't know yet that you can always find that perfect moment right before everything shatters—which was why I said it out loud, like evidence for my side of things. The side, as I saw it at the time, of love.

"But yesterday . . ." I said, "you said I was priceless."

He leaned in and touched my face, and I thought he was going to say, *You are, it's me. You are, and I love you, and my friend is just messing with my head. You are and I just need a break to know for sure. To remember for sure. That we belong.* Only he didn't say any of that. And, while I do believe, even now, he couldn't hear himself clearly—couldn't possibly hear just how bad it sounded coming out—he did say it.

He reached over and touched my face.

"You were," he said.

The allure of "Checking Out"—the reason the column met, from the start, with a certain level of success—was that it gave people a sense of control. They'd learn about a list of things they needed to experience in a certain place: an extraordinary sight ("Take in the view of the Taj Mahal from the Oberoi Amarvilas in Agra"), an extraordinary taste ("Try the special stewed bamboo rolls at the famed T'ang Court in Hong Kong's Central District"), discovering the one thing that couldn't be found anywhere else ("Don't forget to buy a hundred sheets of freshly made paper from the only operating paper factory in Amalfi—it's been going since 1592!"). They did these things, enjoyed them, took photographs of themselves enjoying them— and then they got to feel like they'd not only experienced that place, but had truly broken away from their real lives. Next!

Only, as my editor, Peter W. Shepherd, said to me not too long ago, "If I may quote Steinbeck"—Peter was British and about a hundred years old and one of my very favorite humans, but since he began working on his novel (which he described as *"Tortilla Flat,* only British"), he would use any excuse to start a sentence by quoting Steinbeck—Peter said, "'A journey is like marriage. The certain way to be wrong is to think you control it.'"

Of course, whether I liked it or not, he was on to something. There was a faultiness governing "Checking Out." That sense of control was an illusion. The magic of Big Sur, as an example, came from spending a whole day propped up on the rocks by the post office, listening to the ocean behind you. Except that most people didn't have the time or inclination to sit by the post office all day doing nothing. But they could find fifty glorious minutes to head to Bixby Canyon Bridge and the most beautiful intersection of mountain rock and ocean you could ever hope to see. Feel like they had a perfect hegira, check it off their list.

In each of my categories in "Checking Out," I tried to give readers that sense of escaping—of breaking free of their everyday boundaries, of leaving their comfort zone. I labeled the categories with this in mind (I called the sightseeing part of the column "Open Your Eyes" and another part, in which readers were to venture off the beaten path, "Take the Wrong Exit"). And I was very careful not to pick anything too obvious as the thing to see (no Statue of Liberty) or too common as the thing to taste (no sampling the everything pie from Ray's Pizza in the West Village). Finally, I put the most pressure of all on the last category on the list ("Discover the One Thing You Can't Find Elsewhere")—which, in addition to always having to be captivating, had the most important job of all: to make people feel that, after they finished this last one, they were ready to go home again.

In those first days after Nick was gone, I couldn't help but wonder if Nick had done a "Checking Out" column about me, what would he have put in it? And what would be the final thing? This was what I wanted to know most. What was the final thing that helped him decide he'd had the experience of me? And it was okay—it was time now—for *him* to go?

One small blessing was that after Nick broke up with me,

he was the one to go. He left that very afternoon to stay with his family, or his new friend, or the Village People. I didn't ask and Nick didn't offer. What he did say was that he wouldn't come back to the house or call or begin the process of disentangling our lives (our joint bank account, our house, our cars, our shared computer, our one stock) until I was ready. I could call him when I was ready for that. When we were more healed. He'd used that word. *Healed*. It is a miracle, when I let myself think about it, that I didn't slap him.

I was too stunned, right when it happened, to be that angry. Or even that sad. Then I was that sad. I was sadder than I'd ever been. All this time later, the best way that I can describe those first days is that I couldn't do much but lie in bed at night and listen to the creak of the floorboards. And pretty much all day I'd do the same thing. My heart seemed to have moved in my chest—actually managed to move itself—right into a place it didn't belong, where it felt heavy and stuck. I'd lie there, listening to nothing, feeling my heart like that.

Then, on the tenth day, my closest friend, Jordan (aka Jordan Alisa Riley, international defense attorney, great beauty, asskicker) came barreling into my house, her three-year-old daughter, Sasha, in tow. Jordan used her key, which meant I didn't get much of a warning, just a loud hello. A loud, *We're here.*

Jordan and I had been best friends since week one of our freshmen year of college when we were placed in dorm rooms next door to each other. Her roommate was crazy (there was a shrine to *Saved by the Bell* involved). So by week two of freshmen year, Jordan was pretty much living in my dorm room. The rest was our history. Our lovely and loving history. We knew each other so well by this point—knew each other in that honest, unmitigated way that people get to know you who meet you when you're still young. Before all the rest of it. Before it becomes both easier and harder to know yourself.

As an example, Jordan and I knew each other so well that on the morning of day ten, post-Nick, I got up and showered, "dressing up" in jeans and a purple tank top. Because even though she hadn't called, I knew she'd be coming, and I wanted her to see that I was okay when she got there. Purple equaled okay in my mind. Sad, pathetic people didn't wear purple. They wore black. Or maybe green.

This was also the reason that I was sitting at the kitchen table, pretending to be working. I did it for Jordan. I figured it would make her worry about me less. And, as a bonus, I thought it'd be a good message to be sending in case she happened to speak to Nick.

Because there was that too: Jordan was Nick's sister.

We had met—Nick and I—at Jordan's and my college gradu-ation. Nick liked to say that he fell in love with me then, gradu-ation day, the first time he saw me. I always doubted that story. For one thing, we didn't start dating until a few years later. For another, a cap and gown isn't the best look for anyone.

Jordan stood in the kitchen doorway, her arms on her hips as she studied me.

"Well, the good news is," she said, "you're tiny. You've lost six pounds, maybe seven . . ."

I pushed back from my chair and got up to hug her, wrapping my arms tightly around her neck, Sasha holding on to both my legs. Jordan, meanwhile, was crying. She was crying harder than I was, which was disconcerting. Jordan wasn't the sentimental type. Not soft. Though she did write a letter to the editor every time one of my "Checking Out" columns came out, which I took as proof of her secretly sweet heart. Still, in almost fifteen years of friendship, I had seen her cry exactly twice. This counting as time number two.

"So here's the deal," she said, pulling away and wiping at her tears. "I brought you some of that disgusting kale salad you love from the vegan restaurant in the Palisades."

"You did?" I said.

She nodded. "It smells like turkey in there, by the way, but I got you a pound of the stuff. And a vat of your favorite coffee. So, first things first, we're going to sit down and you're going to eat."

It wasn't exactly a question.

"Okay," I said.

"That's step one. You're going to do that *immediately* before the kale gets even colder and grosser than it is," she said.

"What's step two?" I asked.

"You'll see."

....

We sat at the kitchen table, Sasha coloring in her Wonder Woman Coloring Book, Jordan and I sitting next to each other, the pound of kale between us. The sun streamed through the windows, spotlighting the kale, making it look more than a little like kryptonite.

As I poured myself some coffee, Jordan picked up a piece of kale, smelled it, and put it back down.

"Well," she said, "I've been waiting patiently for you to call, but I have to go to Italy tomorrow for work, and I couldn't wait any longer."

I took a sip, and tried to think of how to say it. "I didn't want to put you in the middle."

"Put me in the *middle?*" Jordan leaned closer toward me, made me meet her eyes. "What is this middle you speak of? For the record, I hate my brother for this."

"For the record," I said. "I'm not crazy about him either, at the moment."

"He's obviously gone insane. That's number one. And this Pearl person?"

Pearl. She had a name. It was Pearl.

Jordan shook her head, sitting back in her chair. "I never

liked her, even when I *knew* her," she said. "She grew up down the street from us. Did Nick tell you that?"

"Not exactly." I paused, not wanting to ask—and having to ask. "What was she like?" I said.

"A hundred years ago? The head cheerleader, the homecoming queen, the nightmare of every girl whose boobs came in late."

"Fantastic."

"So what?" Jordan said, disgust in her voice. "She's also bossier than me and that's saying something! And *Pearl?* Seriously? Who's even named that under the age of ninety?"

"I think one of the baristas over at Caffe Luxxe is named Pearl and she's definitely in her twenties, maybe her early thirties . . ."

Jordan put up her hand to stop me. "The point is, Nick's a nutjob if he thinks this is okay by me. He asked if we could all have dinner next Sunday. I said, 'That sounds great. In a world where *great* means the worst invitation anyone has ever offered me.'"

I laughed, which made Sasha look up and smile. Her smile matched Jordan's—same curving of the lower lip, same half giggle behind it—which was somewhat surprising considering that Jordan was technically Sasha's stepmother. But in a way it made perfect sense. Jordan loved Sasha as though as she was her own, it often seemed. The other time I'd seen Jordan cry? When Simon had taken Sasha to visit his folks in Martha's Vineyard. Jordan hadn't gone because of work. That was that last time she'd chosen to be apart from Sasha because of anything.

"Bottom line? As far as I'm concerned, Nick has less than five minutes to get the h-e-l-l over himself and stop being a c-l-i-c-h-é."

I looked at Sasha, who was coloring again. "Why are you spelling c-l-i-c-h-é?"

She sighed. "I don't know. I got carried away."

I squeezed her hand.

"It just makes me mad, you know?" she said. "And this is not me defending him, *believe me*. But between Facebook and BBM and every other type of technology that makes you two clicks away from *anyone* in the universe, nowadays you've got to try *not* to get emotionally involved with someone new. You have to try *not* to reach out to an old fling and start shrieking about *maybe we're meant to be*. You know what I'm saying?"

I shook my head. "I can't say I do."

She gave me a look. "I'm saying hazy is the new black," she said. "All this pseudo-hiding-behind-computer-banter in the name of love . . . it makes me sick. What happened to the good old days when cheating meant actually cheating?"

I stood up, gathering the plates to bring them to the sink. "Jord, I need you to hear me, okay? Nick loves you more than anything in the world. You're his best friend too. Don't be mad at him on my account. He hasn't actually done anything wrong. I think he left so he wouldn't. That's fair. It's not fun or anything, but it's fair. Plus, I'm not innocent in this. I'm away all the time, as he'll gladly tell you."

"Excuse me?"

"I'm just saying he has a point. It's hard to maintain a good relationship with someone who's not around. And I've always been like that, right? I moved twelve times before I even turned eighteen, and now I travel half the year for work." I shrugged. "I don't think in my whole life I've been in the same place for more than a week."

Her eyes opened wide, as though she understood something for the first time. "Oh, I see! So it's your fault that your mother is a lost loon, and that Nick is having an early midlife terror attack? Both of those things are on you?"

Before I could answer, she started looking around the room. Then she turned back to me.

"Where's the dog?" she said.

"What does that have to do with anything?"

"You let him take the *fucking* d-o-g?" she asked.

"You spelled the wrong word," I said.

"You *love* Mila. In that gross, irritating way where people talk about you behind your back."

"So does Nick."

She gave me a stunned look, but I turned away. How could I explain it, anyway? Even now, after Nick had caused me pain, the truth was I didn't want to cause him any. Wasn't that love, after all?

Jordan turned toward her daughter, shaking her head. "Sasha, do you believe this?" she asked. "Your aunt is being loyal to a *man* even in the face of his questionable moral character. Don't do that. In fact, that is what not to do. When you grow up and some guy is being bad, you turn on him like the wind. Understood?"

Sasha kept coloring, smiling at her Wonder Woman creation, Wonder Woman's costume now entirely bright orange.

"Acknowledge that you hear me, baby," she said.

"I acknowledge, Mommy," she said. Then she picked up a different crayon, a new shade of orange, and started on Wonder Women's hair.

Jordan kissed Sasha on the forehead, pushing her soft curls back away. Then she kissed her again.

"So here's what I'm thinking . . ." she said, turning back to me. "And I don't want to hear any arguments."

I sat back down, giving her a smile. "That's shocking."

"You're going to come with us to Venice, until the dust clears. I have an embezzlement case there that should last twelve weeks or so. We're getting a great house walking distance to the Rialto. Right by the single best coffee shop in the world. And, as no small bonus, *this* Venice," she motioned around herself, "will feel a million miles away."

"That sounds amazing," I said.

"Great. Then it's settled."

I shook my head. "I have to work," I said.

"I'm sorry, don't they have computers in Italy?" she asked.

I didn't have a good answer, but I wanted her to understand how impossible it felt to take her up on her offer. "I can't walk away from my life right now."

"Annie, I think it walked away from you already," she said.

I drilled her with a look.

"Not helpful?" she said. "I'm sorry. I suck at this. I just don't want this to get as bad as it might get."

"What's that supposed to mean?" I asked, even though I knew. I wasn't one of those women who moved on quickly: had a new boyfriend a week later, had a new way of looking at the old one. My "process" was a little less forgiving than that. First I had to blame myself for everything that went wrong. And then everything that didn't.

"Come to Venice, Annie," Jordan said. "Nick will get over this. Life will go back to normal. In the meantime, let's have some fun! Be the opposite of you."

Be the opposite of you: those words hit me, right away, penetrating the fog. *Be the opposite of me?* It was day ten and this was the first thing I remember hearing that sounded like a good idea. It was the first thing that sounded something like a real plan. For getting on with it.

"It would help me out too," Jordan continued. "Simon and I can actually spend a little time alone. Have a romantic dinner, occasionally. Go for a long walk." She paused. "See? This isn't even about your needs. I'm basically using you for child care."

I laughed. "I don't know, Jordan. . . ."

"Yes. You do." She looked right at me. "We both know Nick's coming back to you. It's just the five-year itch. That's a very real thing. I plan to be in Morocco for mine. Speaking of which,

I'm going to need some hotel recommendations when the time comes. Something with a spa."

I shook my head. "It's not that simple," I said.

"It is. But I'll grant you that your five-yearer came at the worst *possible* time. Nick just got his first taste of fame and has temporary amnesia that he is a nerdy guy who . . ." Her eyes went wide, something occurring to her. "Stopped wearing his nerdy-guy glasses."

"So?" I said.

"So, I should've known something was going on when he started wearing those contact lenses. How did I miss it?" She shook her head. "It's like he took his *brain* off when he took those glasses off. It's all very Piggy in *Lord of the Flies*."

I looked at her, confused. "Piggy's glasses were broken, I think."

She waved me off. "You're missing the point," she said.

"Which is what?"

"That Nick loves you. He loves you so much that I can guarantee nothing *real* is going to happen with Pearl. But men can forget. If too much time goes by, they can forget what they have. How much they *want* what they have. And you shouldn't suffer while he remembers. I won't allow it." She paused. "Besides, the sooner you aren't, the sooner he'll be back. That's the way it works."

That part I couldn't help but agree with. It seemed to me that the universe was tricky that way—as soon as you didn't need something as badly, as soon as you hold onto the hope of it less tightly, you get a second shot at it.

I put my forehead against hers. "I love you," I said. "In case you didn't know."

"So come to Venice with me. And, just this once, let someone be the one that takes care of you."

"Your brother says he has been," I said. "Too much."

She sighed. "I really *wish* you'd stop referring to him that way."

I smiled. "I'll think about coming," I said. "I really will."

"No you won't."

"Maybe not." I said. "But no more doomsday talking, okay? I promise you, I'll be *fine*. Look at me. I *am* fine. And to prove it, this time tomorrow I begin again. What's five years, anyway? Forget tomorrow. Tonight, I head outside and rejoin the world. I already have plans. *Big* ones. . . ."

She sat back in her chair. "My God, you're a terrible liar," she said. "It's amazing to watch, actually."

"Where did I lose you? The I-already-have-plans bit?"

She grabbed my pinky, giving it a tight squeeze.

"Yeah, that part could have used some work," she said. "Plus, your purple tank top is inside out."

After Jordan left that night, I cried myself to sleep.

This was what I was up against: five Christmases and five New Years, ten birthdays, and every Thanksgiving. Six cross-country trips, three half-country ones, three movie sets, one ten-year college reunion. Two trips to the hospital for food poisoning, one car accident in Mexico, three broken bones, one appendicitis. Five grandparents' (and step-grandparents') deaths. Valentine's Day in Hong Kong, Valentine's Day in New York City, Valentine's Day barely speaking to each other in the same house. His sister's wedding, *two* of my mother's divorces, four mutual godchildren, one angel of a chocolate Labrador retriever. A shared language, a shared family, a shared future plan to travel the world together. Two weeks on a terrible houseboat near Lake Michigan, the last night when he gave me a locket anyway, four small words on the back, as if they made perfect sense: *For you, for always.* Not one day when we didn't talk, even if it was to argue. Not one night when I didn't say good night, even if I didn't mean it. Not one morning when the first thing I didn't think was, *You.*

Then I woke up in the middle of the night, remembering something else. I remembered a trip we took toward the beginning of our relationship, six months in, when we went to Utah for a long weekend. The first night we were there, we were staying at an old rustic cabin outside Moab, right outside town, and before we went to sleep, I said, "How is this so easy?"

"We should enjoy it while it lasts," Nick said. "I'm guessing it won't always be this easy . . ."

I must have looked distraught. He tried to rectify it immediately—moving closer to me, comforting me by saying he spoke glibly—that it would be this easy between us always, or close to this easy. Of course it would. But, the problem was, *easy* wasn't the word that had caused me distress.

It was the *always*.

A small, inexplicable part of me was scared, right from the start—of counting on someone, of trusting that he'd always be there for me—as much it was exactly what another part of me wanted.

And I wondered how I had gotten here.

4

It wasn't the next night, but the night after that when I decided I'd keep my promise to Jordan: I'd rejoin the land of the living. A little after five, I turned on the radio, took a piping-hot shower, and put on my makeup. Movement seemed key, so I didn't stop to think about any of it too much. Hair drying and brushing, dangly earrings on. It felt a little like watching a video of myself when I caught a glance of my face in the mirror: *Hello, aren't you someone I used to know?*

Picking out something to wear turned out to be easier than anticipated, because I hadn't done laundry since Nick's exit and there were precisely two articles of clothing left hanging in our closet: a hot-pink kimono that I had gotten at a flea market in Camden Town, which, among its other problems—like the fact that it was a hot-pink kimono—was two sizes too small. And then there was my yellow dress. Wrapped in dry-cleaner's plastic: protected, ready. I usually reserved it for weddings or black-tie events, as I lived in fear of ruining it. It was my magic dress, as Jordan called it. The kind of dress that makes you four inches taller and ten pounds lighter, *and* makes your boobs look bigger. In this lifetime, if we are lucky, we each get one.

And that night it was all I had.

I sat down on my bed to put on my red, strappy peep-toes and to figure out where I could go that I'd be dressed somewhat appropriately. My usual bar, down on Abbot Kinney, didn't feel like a candidate. The fanciest person in there would be wearing a clean T-shirt.

So I decided I would drive down Ocean Avenue into Santa Monica, head to one of my favorite local escapes: a small, fancy hotel on the beach where I could sit at one of the tables on the patio, one of the five tables that gives you a view of the nicest sunset you've ever seen. A view that could send you a hundred miles away from anything resembling real life.

This was the plan: a removal from real life. For the evening, at least. Until I fell asleep before putting the plan into action. Right there, on the bottom half of the bed, in my magic dress.

I don't remember lying down. But, when I woke up, I had one peep-toe sandal half on, my magic dress was wrinkled, and it was 12:21 A.M., which may as well have been 4:00 A.M., Los Angeles time. Most everything was shut down for the night, or well on its way to getting there. Including my beach-fancy hotel restaurant and bar. I got up anyway, grabbed my other sandal, and—before I could talk myself out of it—picked up my car keys and headed out the front door. Maybe part of it was that I wanted to be able to tell Jordan I did something constructive, or maybe it had less to do with Jordan than I understood even then, some force I couldn't explain already at work.

All I know is that when I walked into the restaurant and saw those twelve-foot windows leading out to the beach and the ocean and the rest of everything, it didn't matter that the lights were down, and that the place was empty, the patio furniture long put

away, the music—Bruce Springsteen's "The Fever," I believed—
on low. Or that the sole living person still inside was a guy with
curly hair: standing behind the bar, wiping it down.

The problem was that the guy with the curly hair behind
the bar wasn't the normal bartender—the one who I'd become
friendly with over the years, friendly enough that Nick and I had
helped him read through lines one night for a sitcom audition
he had the next day—and who I guessed was my best shot of
getting a drink so late.

I walked over to him. "You're not Ray," I said.

I must have sounded seriously disappointed because this guy
laughed.

"No," he said. "I guess I'm not."

He gave me a smile, big and round, and I felt grateful that
the first words out of his mouth weren't the obvious ones: *We're
closed.* Then I noticed his face. He had a nice face—a strong
jaw, wide-open eyes, a blond scruff of beard matching his silly-
looking curls. A significant dimple, making its way confidently
through that scruff. He was also wearing a green jacket that
matched his eyes a little too perfectly.

"Does that mean I'm too late for last call?" I asked.

"Officially or unofficially?" he asked, taking a final swipe at
the countertop.

"Whichever answer gives me the best shot of getting a bourbon straight up," I said. "Pinch of salt."

This was when he smiled again. It was a knock-you-out smile—
this close to being too smooth for its own good. But it redeemed
itself because it also seemed another way: nervous, genuine. Accidentally smooth. Which, all of a sudden, felt even more dangerous.

He slung the dish towel over his shoulder. "That's my drink
of choice too," he said.

I shook my head. "That's no one's drink of choice *too*," I said.

But then he pulled out a small Riedel glass from behind the

bar, a little bourbon still left in it, the salt line visible. "I had an uncle who used to drink it that way when I was growing up. I guess I just got used to it," he said. "You can have a try, if you like."

Instead I stood up on my tiptoes, and leaned over the bar to have a better look.

"Come on, do you have a hundred different drinks lined up back there, waiting to be pulled out? That's a hell of a way to get tips."

"Would you like to have a seat?" He motioned toward the empty bar stool directly in front of him, gestured for me to take it.

"Really?" I said, as if it were up for debate. As if I weren't already taking it eagerly—my dress hiking up too high on my legs, as I positioned myself as close to the bar as possible, trying to get comfortable.

I guess I was moving a little awkwardly because he was looking at me more than slightly confused. "You all right, there?"

"I'm good," I said. I held out my hand, still just trying to seem friendly, get that drink. "I'm Annabelle . . . though pretty much everyone calls me Annie. Adams."

He reached out to take my hand, but before he could, I heard footsteps and we both turned to see a familiar face. It was Ray, the usual bartender, in his street clothes, walking toward us. He had a leather jacket slung over his shoulder.

"Griffin, I'm outta here, my man . . ." Ray said. Then he interrupted himself, noticing me. "Hey, I know you. It's Samantha, right? Samantha in the pretty dress?"

I smiled. "Close," I said.

"Ray, this is Annie Adams," the guy behind the bar said. Griffin, apparently.

Ray looked back and forth between us. "Well, Annie Adams, in the pretty dress, I actually closed out for the night already. Sorry about that. Show starts again at four P.M. tomorrow. . . ."

I started to stand, but, before I could, Griffin put his hand on top of mine, gently, stopping me exactly where I was.

"That's cool, Ray, Annie's a friend of mine. I dragged her out to have a nightcap with me while I finish up some things. Go on, I'll lock it out for you."

Ray looked back at me. "You're friends with Griff?" he said.

I smiled at *Griff*, as he poured me my bourbon, a double shot of it, the greatest amount of salt going in, right on top.

"Absolutely," I said.

"Cool, then." Ray twirled his leather jacket over his head and turned to leave. "Later!"

When I looked back at Griffin, he was holding up his bourbon glass, tipping it toward me. "I'm guessing you're glad I'm not Ray now."

"Very," I said, tipping mine toward him.

Then I took a long, slow sip of the bourbon. It felt warm and right hitting my throat.

"That is a pretty dress though," he said. "He's right about that."

I shrugged. "Don't let it fool you," I said. "It's a magic dress."

"I don't . . ." He shook his head. "I don't get it."

"It's like a mirage. But all I had was this and a very pink kimono, and the kimono doesn't fit me anymore." I paused. "Really, to be honest with you, I'm not sure it ever did."

He started to laugh—this was funny? Apparently this was funny.

Griffin walked around the bar and pointed at the bar stool next to mine.

"May I?" he asked. "It'll make it seem more believable that we actually know each other."

"In case Ray comes back?" I asked, and smiled.

He smiled back, his dimple growing. "Exactly," he said.

I patted the bar stool. "Be my guest," I said.

He sat down and pulled his long legs around, so we were facing each other. And I noticed that the jacket he had unbuttoned—the bright green jacket—was a chef's jacket. The words EXECUTIVE CHEF embroidered over the pocket, in white.

"Wait a minute, *you're* the chef here?"

He looked down at his jacket, and pulled on the lettering. "I am?" he joked, responding to how surprised I sounded. "Wow, I guess so, if that's what the jacket says."

"Sorry . . . I just . . . you were standing back there so I thought you worked here as a bartender. As your day job. Or your night job, I guess. I thought maybe you were an actor."

"What would make you think that?"

I didn't know how to make *your eyes for starters* sound like a noncreepy answer.

"Apparently I make up stories," I said.

He smiled. "Well, the last time I stepped on a stage was for my fifth-grade class's production of *The Pajama Game*."

"I love *The Pajama Game*," I said.

"You wouldn't have liked this version of it. Trust me."

I gave him a smile. "And now you're the chef here?"

He nodded. "Temporarily, at least. The regular chef, Lisa, is off for the next few months on maternity leave. I'm just filling in. I used to be the chef at their sister restaurant in the Berkshires. A place called Maybelline's. It's about twenty miles outside Stockbridge."

"I know Stockbridge. I just went there last year. Or pretty close to there, at least. Great Barrington, actually. I was there for work. If I had known, I'd have gone to your restaurant and written about it. I'm a travel writer. I write this column called 'Checking Out.' But I was only allowed to write about Great Barrington. That was what the column was about. So I guess I couldn't have written about you. Not that time. . . ."

I started to fade out, in spite of myself, and Griffin tilted his head, like he was wondering if he was missing something again.

"Sorry," I said. "I'm just a little sleep-deprived these days. It's making me over . . . talk."

He reached over and held his fingers close to my cheek, not

touching my cheek but incredibly close to it. "But you have sleep marks," he said. "Right there."

I felt a chill. I felt a chill right where he could have touched me. I reached my hand up, instinctively, covering that side of my face. "Those are complicated," I said.

He laughed. "I'm sure they are," he said.

"So you're no longer at Maybelline's?"

"No, I'm actually opening my own restaurant in Williamsburg next winter. When I get back to Massachusetts. . . ."

I looked at him confused, wondering if I'd misheard. "Did you say Williams*town?*" I asked, thinking of the charming town in the Berkshires. Home of the amazing summer theater festival. Home of the Clark Art Institute. Home of one of my first "Checking Out" columns.

"No, Williams*burg.* But everyone hears Williamstown, you're not alone in that," he said. "It's about an hour from there. In the Pioneer Valley. I grew up in Williamsburg, actually, which is why I'm opening the restaurant there."

I smiled. "That's exciting."

He smiled back. "Glad to hear you think so. Then you can come back and write about my new place. In exchange for these drinks."

"Deal," I said.

He reached over the bar top, picked up the bottle of bourbon, and poured each of us some more, placing the bottle on the counter between us when he was done. I couldn't help but stare at the bottle, which was losing its liquid considerably fast.

"So," he said. "Care to elaborate?"

I looked up at him confused.

"The sleep marks. Their complications?"

"Oh." I shrugged, trying to think of how to say it. "I'm not exactly myself these days," I said.

Griffin took a long drink of his bourbon, as if contemplating this. When he did, I noticed a tattoo on his wrist—a tattoo of an anchor, or half of an anchor, the circle tilt at the bottom abruptly cut off.

And this was the first thing I did, the first thing that proved the point that I wasn't exactly myself: I touched it. I touched the tattoo, running my fingers along its edges. Why should this have been normal? And yet, somehow, it was. Griffin had no reaction. He just looked down at his wrist, watched how my finger was running along where the tattoo abruptly cut off, the unfinished part. The minus part.

"There's a story behind this," he said. "Though I'm not sure it's a very good one."

"It involves an old girlfriend?" I asked.

"Yes. It involves an old girlfriend, my eighteenth birthday, and a long night at a tattoo parlor in Canada."

"Did you guys think it would be a good idea to share? Kind of like a best friend necklace?"

He shook his head, pointing at me.

"See?" he said. "This is exactly why I have my rule about talking about other women with the one in front of me."

"And what's that?"

"I don't do it."

I laughed. "Got it," I said. "But what happens when a new girlfriend wants to know about an ex? About your relationship history with the girls who came before. How do you cover that territory?"

"She gets to know two pieces of information. The best thing. And the worst. The rest? People think it makes them closer to know everything, but I'm not sure it's fair."

I poured myself a topper, trying to figure that out. "To the person you used to be with?"

"To everyone. It's like living in the past, and not even in an accurate version of it. We only really remember things for five years. After that, what we remember, what's actually etched in our brain, is our memory of the thing, not the thing itself. And five years after that, what's left is our memory of the memory. You follow me?"

"Enough so that I'm getting a little depressed," I said.

He smiled, and it occurred to me—it was one objectively true thing—that smile could bring you down to your knees.

"Okay, so I'll bite," I said. "Tell me about the tattoo girlfriend. Tell me the best thing and the worst thing."

"Well, the best thing about Gia is . . ."

I smiled. "I like the name Gia," I said.

"Me too," he said. Then he nodded, as if he were thinking about it, thinking that was true. "The best thing about *Gia* was probably the tattoo."

"What was the worst thing?"

He picked up his glass of bourbon, held it to his lips for a minute.

"Same answer," he said.

. . . .

Somehow, we ended up in the kitchen.

This part surprised me, almost more than anything that happened later. We ended up in the kitchen, a little after 3:00 A.M., cooking a vat of scrambled eggs. Or, more accurately, Griffin was cooking the eggs in a very large French skillet. Meanwhile, I was sitting cross-legged on the countertop, next to the stove, facing him. Like it was something we knew how to do. Five hours ago, I hadn't known him. I remember thinking that as I watched him cooking the eggs. I remember thinking that, and thinking that didn't seem possible.

"You're doing those eggs a *lot* like my mother used to," I said, watching him add in milk. Watching the way he stirred.

"These are my specialty," he said.

I shrugged. "My mom wasn't a very good cook."

"Ha-ha," he said.

He reached into a small refrigerator near the stove and took out some cracked lobster claws, a beautiful block of Gruyère.

"Okay, she didn't use those things," I said.

"Wait until you taste the final product," Griffin said.

He took off his chef's jacket and rolled up the sleeves of his shirt in a jokey fashion, as though he was really getting down to business. But then something fell out of his jeans pocket: a small red asthma bronchodilator. He bent down to pick it up off the floor, put it back in.

I pointed at the floor, at the spot where the inhaler had fallen. "You have asthma?"

He nodded. "Since I was a kid," he said.

"Any big problems?"

He shook his head. "Not since I was a kid."

"My second stepfather's son has asthma. When he'd come to visit, he'd always carry around a blue bronchodilator. I'd steal it and pretend it was mine. I kind of thought it was cool. To suck the air in . . ."

I made a gesture with my hands, which knocked me a bit off balance—and was my first clue as to how much the bourbon had started affecting me.

"You need a hand?" he asked.

"I've got it together," I said. "Or pretty much together, at least. Which is no small miracle to tell you the truth."

"Why's that?"

"I did something terrible that involves watching a certain movie that I love, and now I'm facing the consequences."

"Which movie's that?"

"*Roman Holiday.*"

He was quiet for a minute, as he finished adding in the lobster and the cheese. "Are you usually this honest?" he asked.

"No never. Never in the history of my life," I said. Then I added, "Sorry about that."

"Don't be. I agree with you."

"Agree with me about what?" I said.

"*Roman Holiday*'s a really great movie," he said.

I smiled.

Griffin took the pan off the still-going burner, and scooped out a large forkful of the eggs, blowing on it, slowly and deliberately, before holding it out for me to take the first bite.

"You may want to brace yourself," he said.

"I'm braced," I said.

Then I took a bite of the eggs and realized how *unbraced* I was.

They were totally and completely delicious. The single most delicious thing I'd ever tasted. I'd tasted all sorts of things that had competed for that ranking—a mustard-coated prime rib in Salzburg, Germany; blowfish in Kyoto; chocolate-covered crickets in Nova Scotia—but nothing like these eggs. How do you describe something that good? They tasted like cotton candy, but the egg version. They were creamy and rich and melted as soon as they touched my tongue, as soon as I tasted the sea-salty edge of them.

And maybe it was in part the bourbon, and maybe it was in part that I hadn't really had an appetite since Nick left. But I don't think so. I don't think those parts were the important ones. Not then. The important one was this: if I could have dived right into the pan, I seriously would have considered doing it.

Instead, I scooped up another enormous bite.

Griffin smiled, knowing he had me. I attempted a shrug. "Not bad," I said, my mouth full.

"Not bad? They are fucking *great*."

I laughed. "They are," I said. "They are fucking great."

"Thank you for that," he said. "And if you ever do make that trip back to western Mass., I might even go up to Lasse's Seafood Mart and get us the real deal. You've never seen lobster claws so red. Lasse makes you work for them, though. He only sells the *really* good stuff to the local chefs at three A.M., sometimes later, sometimes closer to four A.M., a little before he goes out lobstering with his son. And even then, he only sells them if he is in a good enough mood. And then, only to the chefs he can stand."

"That seems unnecessary."

He smiled. "You haven't tasted those lobster claws," he said.

Then he took another fork out of the drawer and jumped up on the countertop so he was sitting cross-legged too, directly in front of me, the pan between us. I tried to move all of the eggs to my side of the pan, breaking off just a small portion for him.

"Um . . ." I said. "Get your own pan."

He fought a smile, that dimple making a final appearance as he waited for me to relent.

"Fine," I said, and shuffled one more biteful to his side of the pan. "But you leave me no choice. I'm cutting you off after this."

"How generous," he said. Then he tilted his head, and looked at me. Really looked.

"So, how are you dealing with it?" he asked.

"With what?"

I was smiling, looking down at the eggs, stuffing another less-than-ladylike bite into my mouth.

"Whatever the movie brought on."

I met his eyes and felt myself get serious for a minute—made myself swallow, hard. "I'm trying to be the opposite of myself," I said.

I didn't offer further explanation. I waited for him to ask for one, or compliment me—say that, from the little he knew, I seemed okay the way I was. But he did something better.

"Anything I can do to help?" he asked.

This was when I kissed him.

5

I learned an important lesson from "Checking Out" about how and why people travel far from home—far from where they started. There was, of course, the obvious reason: escape. Escape from the monotony of every day. So many of us chasing what we wished our everyday existence could be instead. But there was a less obvious and perhaps more important reason. Somewhere, often right in the middle of a trip, you got to believe this *was* your everyday life. You got to believe you were never going home again.

When I woke up at Griffin's the next morning, it took me a moment to realize I wasn't home. It took less than that to realize I didn't want to go back. Not yet. I didn't want to go back to how I was feeling there. And so I didn't move. I stayed lying there, fairly frozen—feigning sleep—in Griffin's bed.

He, meanwhile, was walking around the apartment, already in his jeans, no shirt on, trying to get it together before his twelve-hour shift started.

The hotel had given him very nice digs, a suite on the top floor of the hotel: Ralph Lauren furnished, sandy beach views, ocean views beyond that. But all I was looking at was Griffin, in front of me, still half naked, trying not to reveal that I was thinking of him completely naked. Thinking of him, thinking of me completely naked. I couldn't help but blush, like a teenager. Worse than a teenager. A tween.

I looked away, covering my reddening face, pretending to still be asleep. But it was no use. I was caught—and Griffin was on his way over to sit down next to me on the edge of the bed. I pulled the sheets up higher, trying to gauge how weird it would be if I pulled them over my entire head.

"You're awake," he said.

I nodded, sheet over my chin.

He squinted his eyes, as if thinking about something. Then, instead of offering it up, he gave me a smile.

"So I'm off tomorrow, which is the good news," he said. "What do you say you come surfing with me? I know a great place up near Malibu. A place worth seeing. And if it goes well, I'll take you dancing after."

I couldn't help but smile back at him. "Oh . . . so I'm being tested now?" I said.

"What, you think you're a shoo-in or something?"

"If not, I'm about to fail," I said. "I don't surf."

"But you like dancing, right?" he said.

"Very much . . ." I said. "I like it very much."

And my smile disappeared. Because I did. I loved dancing. But Nick never took me. The thought of going made me so happy, and then so sad, almost simultaneously, because I couldn't help but think that this person I barely knew, he was the one willing to give it to me.

"Weren't you saying something about being the opposite of yourself?" he asked, teasing me.

I was.

"So surfing and then dancing. Tomato, then tomah-to. Do we have a deal?" he asked.

We did.

6

"It's just dinner, right?" I said.

I was looking in the mirror, checking myself out in my little yellow bikini. It was the only bathing suit I could find—and it wasn't the one I'd wanted to find. While it was decent on the top— it had that Marilyn Monroe–like quality to it, the halter hugging at the right place on my neck—that didn't, *couldn't*, make up for the way it curved up fiercely in the behind region, revealing too much of my backside. Plus, ironically, and not in a good way, it was the same exact shade of yellow as my magic dress.

"It's *just* dinner," Jordan repeated back to me.

She was on the other end of the phone, lying on the couch with Simon in Venice, the other Venice. Occasionally I could hear him murmur something in the background, trying to help out—not because he particularly cared, but so she would get off the phone and they could go back to watching their movie for the night. That had been their plan, to watch AFI's top hundred movies while they were away. Tonight they were on *Stagecoach*. If I thought he could hear me, I would've told Simon what he already secretly knew: regardless of when Jordan and I got off the phone, it was over for them and that movie.

"Actually," I said, "it's not just dinner. It's a whole day that includes a beach and . . . travel."

"One date. With the rebound guy," she said. "That's good for everyone. *You're going.*"

"It involves me wearing a bathing suit."

She paused. "That is a little cruel," she said. "Have you been to YogaHop recently?"

I could hear Simon in the background, talking: *Hasn't she already been naked with the guy? Isn't that what you've been gabbing about for the last twelve hours?*

And suddenly, Jordan's voice got distant, further away. I imagined she covered the telephone's receiver in order to answer him, but I could still make out her muffled voice: *That,* she said, *is a completely different thing than swimwear.*

"Exactly!" I shouted. "Thank you, Jordan! Thank you for getting it."

I started to undo the top of my bikini, my fingers working their way through the knot, but then Jordan was back on the phone.

"You're going," she said.

. . . .

Griffin picked me up in a 1957 Chevy pickup truck. Bright blue with light-duty wheels. A small white line of visible paint along the doors. I was sitting on the front steps waiting for him when he drove up.

At first I thought I had imagined it. A 1957 pickup truck was the vehicle I fantasized about. With all the fancy cars in Los Angeles, this was one you'd rarely see, and it was my favorite.

"This is what you drive?" I said.

He was wearing faded jeans and a relaxed T-shirt, and as he

walked around to my side to open the door for me, he looked like an advertisement standing next to the truck. Like an advertisement for a handsome guy.

"What, you like it or something?"

I nodded. "You could say."

He kissed me hello, soft and slow, on my lower lip, like he had done it a thousand times. Like he had the right. The way he pulled it off, he almost did.

"You did say," he said.

I smiled, a little confused. "Wait, what do you mean, I did say?"

"The other night. You told me you loved this truck." He leaned toward me. "So I found one for the afternoon."

"You *found* one?" I said.

"Yes."

I got inside, running my hands along the dashboard. "Where?"

He shrugged. "A shady guy owes me a favor."

I looked up at him. "Really?"

"No, but it sounds cooler than I just rented it from the place the hotel recommended."

I bit my lip, touched. "Thank you," I said. "For risking your life and calling in that favor."

He closed the door behind me, clicked it locked. "Buckle up," he said.

....

During the years that Nick and I had lived in Los Angeles, we had gone to several of the most popular local beaches—Zuma, Manhattan Beach, all the way out to Redondo for a house party. But I had never been to the beach that Griffin took me to that afternoon: El Matador, this cliff-foot strand all the way out on the west side of Malibu. What they call a pocket beach because it's so tiny, so secluded. It was like a vision, with its perfectly white sand and isolated sea caves. We actually had to waddle through the farthest cave, surfboards and equipment in hand, just to get to the spot that Griffin loved most.

"I can't believe how incredible it is here," I said, as he reached into his knapsack. He spread out an oatmeal-colored blanket.

"You never knew about this place?"

I shook my head. "I've been missing out, apparently."

"We'll make up for it," he said. Then he smiled at me, squinting his eyes, tightly. He had forgotten to bring his sunglasses. I reached into my bag and handed him my extra pair. They were on the enormous side, oval-shaped and cherry red. Feminine and ridiculous on him.

"How do I look?"

"Perfect," I said, and smiled.

He handed me a wet suit, the legs folded awkwardly. "You'll need to change," he said.

I stared at it. "You brought me a wet suit?"

He nodded. "It would appear so."

"You brought me a wet suit, but you forgot your sunglasses?"

"You're stalling," he said.

I pointed my finger at him. "But . . . see . . . I thought when you said we were going surfing, and I told you I haven't surfed, you would understand that *that* meant you would surf and I would lie here on the blanket."

"What fun is that?" he said.

I think not drowning is a blast, I wanted to say. But, all of a sudden, I couldn't say it—because I could picture it, as clearly as if Nick were the one standing in front of me. I could picture him laughing at that. It almost made me fall down. I was suddenly and completely inundated by it. What had been lost in losing him.

I sat down on the blanket, trying to catch my breath. And trying to get a hold of my balance before I made a fool of myself.

Griffin bent down, so he was leaning on his knees, standing

over me. "We should probably do it already," he said. "Just get it over with."

I looked at him. "What's that?"

He sat down on the blanket, getting comfortable, holding up his index finger. "One," he said.

"One?"

"One conversation in which you tell me everything you want about him and then we never have to talk about him again."

"Just like that? Throw him out with the bathwater?" I joked. Then, I tried to say what I really meant. "I feel a little weird talking about him," I said.

"I get that." He nodded. "But don't. You're talking about him more by not talking about him."

He was right. But, in a place where I was trying to be reductive, I didn't know where to begin or end. So I sat there quietly, the beach heat kicking up, its strong breeze pushing my hair out of my face, leaving it bare.

"How about if instead of going into everything, I tell you the best thing about him and the worst thing?" I said.

He smiled. "Oh, so now you just want to make fun of me," he said. "Fair enough . . ."

"No." I shook my head. "I'm not. I'm really not making fun. Maybe you're having an influence."

"Okay," he said. "Then go ahead."

"Well," I said. "The best thing is that we'd camp together. We both traveled so much for work, me especially, but when we were home, sometimes Nick would get back from work at the end of the day and we'd put a tent in the backyard, and sleep outside. It sounds silly, I know, but we'd end up staying up most of the night talking, locked into one sleeping bag, watching the sun come up together. It made me happy. And it made me feel safe."

Griffin smiled bigger, not threatened, not with any sort of judgment. "That is a good thing," he said.

I nodded.

"What's the worst?"

I looked right at him. "I don't remember really feeling all that safe any other time."

As soon as the words were out, I felt the weight of them. I felt the weight of what I didn't want to know. That I had felt tested so much of the time Nick and I'd been together. And maybe part of that was my doing as much as his—growing out of my desire to keep him happy because I loved him so much, because I wanted his approval. But did the reason matter so much? In the end it was the same result. Maybe that was part of the reason I wanted to be away from home so much, so I didn't feel so immediately affected by it. That part of Nick—that final 20 percent—that always seemed so out of my reach.

Griffin took my hand, kissed it fast, right on the wrist, and pulled me to standing. One motion.

"Let's get in the water," he said.

"Wait, that's it? We're not going to discuss this?"

"What's there to discuss?"

Nothing. All of a sudden, I knew. Nothing. Or, I should say, I felt nothing. The anxiety in my chest, that tight ball, smaller. Benign. Because there was no denying it. It hadn't just been there since the breakup. It had been there for a while before that. And maybe now—maybe in this instance with Griffin—I was breaking free of it.

"But what about you?" I asked. "Shouldn't you tell me the same thing? About your last girlfriend?"

But Griffin was already removing my bikini top.

"What are you doing?" I asked.

"Getting you into your wet suit."

His hands felt cold and good against my back, chilling me as he removed the straps. I started looking around the beach—there was another couple far out of the way, and a few surfers in the ocean. But, in this part, we were alone. We were completely alone.

"Don't worry," he said. "I won't watch."

Then he did.

....

That night, as promised, we went dancing. I changed into a silver bubble skirt and a silky tank top and put on my tango shoes—yes, I have a pair of special shoes I tango in—which were black and wiry and tied tight right above my ankle.

We danced all night. Every song. Until we were both drenched in sweat, clothes clinging, laughing. Griffin wasn't the best dancer, but he loved the music and was enjoying every second: completely unselfconscious as he twirled me around the floor, wrapped up in the moment with me. This, after a while, started to feel like the same thing.

"Stop putting it off. It's your turn," I said, at one point, while we were taking a break and sharing a ginger ale.

"My turn?"

"I assume I'm not your first love," I said. "Tell me about the girl before me. Best and worst. You know, tit for tat . . ."

He smiled.

"What? I said tit?"

He shook his head. "You said love."

My eyes got wide. "No, I didn't . . . I didn't mean . . ." I shook my head, trying to recover. "Not that I'm *love*. Or not that I'm in love with you. Or that you're in love with me. I meant . . . that's not what I meant."

He grabbed me up to standing, pinning my arms behind my lower back, kissing my neck, holding me there. "The best thing about the last woman I loved," he said, "is that she spoke in full sentences."

"Very funny."

He started pulling me back to the dance floor. "And the worst thing?" I asked. But I was letting myself be pulled, already letting myself forget. "All right, I know where this is going. Same answer."

When you go from amazingly sad (sadder-than-you've-ever-been sad) to happy (singing-in-the-shower happy) in quick succession, it seems like the other was never true. Like when you have a cold and you can't remember that you ever felt normal, or when you feel normal again and, despite having someone sitting right in front of you coughing up a lung, you can't quite feel the sick feeling. You can remember the experience. But holding on to that feeling, that is something else.

It's a little like taking a trip. You find that lift, that lightness again, that you can't believe went missing. Even if you know you left reality. You can't believe—if you hold on to it just right—that your newfound freedom will ever again disappear.

Those first weeks with Griffin, I was happy. I wasn't just a little happy. I was so happy that I could almost forget that somewhere underneath was still a terrible pain. That the happiness was so intense—at least, in part—in response to the pain being incredibly touchable before, and now not.

This led to two things that changed everything.

The first thing was that I got sent away on assignment for

"Checking Out" to Ischia—a small, glorious island on the Tyr-rhenian Sea in Italy. I spent five incredible days getting lost in the romantic gardens of La Mortella, staring at the volcanic slopes of Monte Epomeo, studying honey making with a bee-keeper in Forio, eating that honey straight from her finger.

And when I was on my way back to Los Angeles, I had a feel-ing I couldn't remember having in a long time: I was excited to come home.

Yet when I actually got to my home—to the place that had been my home in Los Angeles—I didn't feel excited anymore. I didn't feel excited and I didn't feel relaxed. I felt something else. Something closer to dread. It took me a minute to realize why. Nick had been there.

It made sense that he would come during a time he knew I'd be away. He had my schedule on his calendar, I knew that—I had put it there.

My problem wasn't that Nick had come to the house. It was his house too. The problem was that he had wanted me to know he had been there. I looked around the kitchen, trying to figure out how I knew this, when I saw it on the kitchen table. He left his coffee mug there. The one I had bought him at Disneyland, a July Fourth weekend a few years back. We'd trudged out there to visit with friends of his from back East who were vacationing with their small kids. It turned out to be a great weekend, one we commemorated with the stupid, enormous mug, a photo-booth photograph of us computer generated on the front. His arms were wrapped around my neck, my mouth in kiss formation—the two of us laughing, glowing, in picture form.

He loved that mug. And he had chosen to take it out of the cabinet and put it on the table. Not to use it—it was unused. But just to take it out and leave it there, for me to find.

I ran my fingers along the mug's rim. My first instinct was to figure it out. Why? What did he want me to know? Was he trying to say he wanted his things? That his trip to another land was turning out to be exactly where he wanted to stay? Or, was he saying his trip away from me was moving closer to over, and he was wanting to come back again? Would I be willing to make that voyage easier for him? Would I be willing to walk him through it—whatever it was that he needed most to feel good about starting over again?

My phone vibrated and I looked down to see I had several missed calls—two from Griffin and one from my editor, Peter. I moved toward the window and looked out over my backyard as I listened to Peter's message.

It always comforted me to hear his voice and picture him, bald and sweet-faced, racing around Manhattan while speaking to me. His message was several minutes long and it seemed like the main purpose was to inform me that our parent company was in the process of being bought out by an even bigger media company. "I just wanted you to hear it from me, so you wouldn't worry too much, my love," Peter said, the New York street noise in the background. "The new publisher is a gentleman of the highest order, and 'Checking Out' is one hundred percent safe. They couldn't be happier. I, on the other hand, am growing quite irritated. My novel is at an impasse, and I had to hear from Nick that you two split? If I may quote Steinbeck here, 'One can find so many pains when the rain is falling.'"

As I disconnected from the voice mail—unable not to wonder for a moment why Nick would take it upon himself to call Peter—the phone vibrated again. It was Griffin, his third time trying to reach me.

I flipped it open. "You don't give a girl much chance to settle in, do you?"

"It's an emergency," he said.

My heart stopped. "What's the emergency?"

"I got tickets to Wilco."

I felt myself start to smile, biting my lip. "And how's that an emergency?" I asked.

"It's in Santa Barbara," he said. "If we want to make it in time to hear 'Remember the Mountain Bed,' we have to leave right now."

I could just shut off the lights, stop asking myself to answer any of Nick's questions, and go.

This was what I did.

....

This was when the other thing happened, the other thing that changed everything: my mother came to town.

My mother came to town and I let Griffin meet her. She was a real estate agent most recently in Scottsdale, Arizona, where she and her newest husband, Gil, had moved about a year and a half ago. She was great at her job (no one knew how to sell a house fast better than my mother did). And she often took trips to celebrate her sales. Though this was the first time a trip had taken her to me.

My mother wasn't exactly easy. And considering the current state of affairs, I might have even tried to avoid seeing her. I was certain she'd have a million questions about how I'd gotten from Nick to Griffin—from the point where she thought she knew what was happening in my life, to a life she didn't know at all. But I felt guilty, knowing she was uncharacteristically worried about me. Plus, Gil was coming with her. Kind and good Gil Taylor. And I decided it might be okay. She seemed to be on better behavior when he was around. We all were.

So we decided to meet at a rustic restaurant in Venice called Gjelina. Griffin and I got there first, and I think he was taken aback when they walked in—or, maybe I should say, when my mother walked in. My mother's beauty could do that. She looked both older and younger than she was: her long blond hair perpetually pulled back in a ponytail, showing off her flawless skin.

Her tired, blue eyes complemented perfectly by a pale blue peasant dress. Knee-high maroon boots.

As she got closer to the table, not exactly smiling, Griffin squeezed my hand.

"Hey hey hey, sweet girl!" Gil said to me, as my mother reached out her hand and introduced herself to Griffin. Griffin, to his credit, didn't just stand up to meet her handshake. He also helped her into her seat.

"It's great to meet you, Mrs. Taylor," he said.

"Oh, let's not start that way. Call me Janet, please," she said, smiling too big, too forcefully. "And it's not Mrs. Taylor, Griffin. Even though that's my beloved's last name. It's Adams. Still just Janet Adams. I kept my name from my marriage to Annie's father. I didn't want to change my name to be different from my daughter's. I'm not built that way. Though if she ever *eventually* marries, I'm sure she won't have any problem changing her name from mine."

There was the other part that Janet chose not to mention. If she had actually changed or hyphenated her name every time she married someone else, it would now be Janet Adams-Samuels-Nussbaum-Taylor. There was an Everett in there too. But that was only for a week. A complicated week in which I turned fourteen and we moved from Boston to Seattle. That time, it was Seattle. And, then, back.

"So we have a new man at the table tonight?" my mom said, settling in. "Did you train him to be so well mannered already? Or is he putting on a show to impress your mother?"

This was vintage Janet. Asking a seemingly innocuous question—one that didn't ostensibly suggest what was beneath it—and there was usually a lot beneath it. We didn't speak very often, but when we did my mother asked questions, *critiqued* in the form of an interested question, so that when you argued, she could say, "What? I was *just* asking."

A prime example: when I decided to become a journalist, she

offered, "That's an surprising decision. Are you sure you want to be stuck behind a desk writing about how other people are exploring the world? What? I was *just* asking." And the first time she met Nick: "He's charming, I suppose, but very devoted to his career. Does that make it hard to maintain a relationship? What? I was *just* asking. . . ."

Yet there we all were, having dinner at Gjelina's, passing around plates of flatbread, drinking too much wine, hearing the details of my mother's plans to rest up on the Mexican coast at a hotel with infinity pools on the edge of cliffs—not the one I recommended in my last column.

At best it was okay—more honestly it was okay *and* stilted, okay *and* slow: the dinner of people trying to act like a family for a night, people who spent the rest of the year not having to act like a family at all.

Griffin was trying, but my mother barely let him try, turning away, cutting him off. It felt like she already voted against him and didn't want any details to get in the way of her feeling good about that vote.

So when he went to the bathroom, I braced myself. I braced myself for what she was going to say, trying to imagine what her problem with him was. He was too thin, too serious, that his pound of blond hair made him look like a four-year-old.

Instead my mother turned to me, her eyes tight on my face. "So this is the new man in your life?" she said. Then: "He certainly does love you, doesn't he?"

I looked up at her, bowled over in surprise. No, that doesn't do it justice. I almost passed out.

"Excuse me?" I said.

She nodded. "It's a lovely thing. A gift, really, when you see love like that. It doesn't happen often."

I had lost the power to speak.

"I can see it in his eyes," she said. "Gil, can't you?"

Gil could.

This was when my mother reached over and took my hand.

"I'm happy for you, baby," she said, squeezing my thumb. "I'm happy for you and I'm happy, selfishly, for me. To get to see you so much . . . like yourself with someone."

It was the single nicest thing she'd ever said to me.

Then, as if remembering herself, she got quiet.

"But shouldn't he wear his hair shorter if he works in a kitchen?" she said. "I mean, is that even sanitary? Does he at least wear a hairnet?"

I shook my head. "I don't know, Mom."

"Shouldn't you at least try to find out?" she said.

I shrugged, shaking my head.

"What? I was *just* asking."

Apparently, she was still my mother.

....

That night, before we fell asleep, Griffin said, in the dark, "Your mother is lovely."

I took my hands off my eyes, tried to see the outline of his face, the moon shining through the bedroom window, that California moon, on a perfect November night.

"My mother is many things, Griffin," I said. "I'm not really sure lovely makes the cut."

With Nick, this is the moment when I would have spun it, when I wouldn't have wanted to walk up the edge of where I was so vulnerable. His family was so picture-perfect: his loving sister, his generous parents, their solid marriage. We would see them regularly, talk to them weekly. I never wanted Nick to know how loaded it was for me with my own family, even in the smallest increments. He didn't seem to want to know that.

But Griffin was waiting. He was still waiting, apparently, for me to say something.

"You're pretty close to your family?" I asked.

"Well, they're certainly not the easiest people in the world, but then again, whose family is?" he said. "And yes. In answer to your question. I'd do anything for them."

I shook my head. "Well, we're not like that. Once my father left, my mother was mostly focused on whoever the new husband was. She tried the best she could, but she just wasn't so focused on me, on our day-to-day life, on making our home . . . a home," I said. "And with all the moving around after that, it was a little like I didn't have one."

"A family or a home?"

"Dealer's choice?" I shrugged. "It's probably why I travel so much now. At least partly. I don't know how to do it another way."

He was quiet for a minute.

"It all may be hard for you to understand. . . ."

"Well, what if I don't try?" he said.

"What do you mean?" I said.

"What if instead of trying to understand all of it, I just agree to be on your mother's side?"

I turned toward him. "Don't you mean my side?"

"No, I mean your mother's side."

"I'm not following . . ." I said.

"I'll just assume that whatever your mother did wrong, she did one thing great. That's you. She figured it out enough to make you. I can overlook the rest. And you can have the freedom to feel whatever you want toward her. With no judgment." Griffin kissed me on the cheek, slow, imprinting me. "I'll still think she's lovely."

I started to cry. It was the most generous thing anyone had ever offered me, and he had done it without even trying.

"That's a nice plan," I told him.

He smiled. "I'm glad we have one."

8

He asked me a month later. Three months to the day from when we first met. Three months. Ninety-one days. The other side of the winter solstice. A season had passed. But only one.

The question didn't start as a proposal. He didn't ask me to marry him at first. First he just asked me to go with him.

"It's coming up," he said. "I have to head back East."

"When?"

"Next week. We've talked about it."

We had. We had talked about it, but I'd avoided thinking about it. January—an entirely different calendar year—had always felt so far away. Where was I going to be in January? I was living in a way that I couldn't think that far ahead. I was living in a way where I couldn't really think.

But now there we were again: sitting at the bar, after hours, two bar stools down from where we had been sitting the first night. Where it all began. People always say that things come full circle, but I think that's not accurate. I think they just come very close. You find yourself almost back where you started, but you've moved slightly. Like evidence of the time that has passed, of the things that have happened. We were, physically, two stools over. And so I could see it, like a recently given-up promise: the image of myself, then, on the bar stool. Hiked up dress. Getting ready for it before I knew I was. The beginning of things.

"Now comes the harder part," Griffin said. "We have to talk about what we're going to do about it."

"What we're going to do about it?" I shook my head. "What can we possibly do about it?"

"I would stay here. I would stay here to see where things go. But I have to get back. I should be back there already, really. I'm finally getting the chance to have my own place. It's what I've always wanted. Right off Main Street by the bookshop and the church." He started to make me a diagram with his hands. "It's a big opportunity for me. And you can write your column from anywhere, right?"

I shook my head. "I can't."

"Why?"

I hadn't said a word about Nick, not a word, not since my best thing/worst thing explanation of us. That was no small miracle. But immediately I thought, *I wish I'd told Griffin. I wish he already knew.* I can't follow someone else somewhere. I had followed Nick across the county, and where had I ended up? I wasn't heading back, just because he was asking me.

Which was when—as if reading my mind—Griffin did something I wasn't expecting. He got down on one knee.

"What are you doing?" I asked.

Then we said this next part at the same time: "This is crazy."

Sometimes you don't know it. What you have been waiting your whole life for. You don't know it until it is happening.

"The thing is I know that we are supposed to be together.

I knew it the second you walked in wearing that dress. . . ." He shook his head. "I can't exactly explain why. Really, I'm not sure I'd want to, even if I could."

He was right. A part of me agreed with him. But it was also crazy. A part of me agreed with that more.

"I will give you an out here if you want it," he said. "I will give you whatever you want. But I don't think we should take it. I think we should be brave here. I think we should start this life right now. Right where we are. . . ."

The words were out of my mouth before I could think about it. When it all started happening—everything that came next— I asked myself: Wasn't that how it was supposed to happen? Wasn't that how it was supposed to begin?

"I can't," I said.

He looked downtrodden, and I felt it in my gut. I had never felt anything exactly like it before. It was like I was hurting myself and he was showing me how it looked. It was right there on his face. How it looked when we listened to our fear. Our uncertainty. When we let it be the thing that guides us. How, even if it may masquerade as safety, it almost always, *ultimately,* does more damage than figuring out how to do something greater, braver. Something bold.

Be the opposite of yourself. Jordan's words rushed back into my head, reannounced themselves to me. Then Nick's did: *Sometimes it feels like you've never really been here, like you couldn't be even if you wanted to be.* Which was when I knew I had to say what I really meant.

I shrugged. "I know it's crazy and impossible and any therapist worth her salt would tell me I'm an insane person. And maybe I am an insane person. Maybe that's true. But I can't, for the life of me, stand here and say no."

He stood up.

This was the way I said yes.

Part 2

....

Happily Ever After

Now, here, you see, it takes all the running you can do, to stay in the same place. If you want to get somewhere else, you must run at least twice as fast as that!

—LEWIS CARROLL

One of the first things "Checking Out" taught me was how amazing the beginning of a trip could be. How there was nothing at all like the realization, early in one's travels, that all options were readily available. A day could be a top-down convertible car ride from Brussels to Amsterdam, or a warm afternoon at Don Alfonso in Sant'Agata sui Due Golfi eating the world's freshest lemon (skin and all), or an evening singing karaoke at the Townhouse in Tokyo. You could make a million choices, or none, and it barely counted yet. It took me time to realize just how invaluable that feeling was—and why.

It isn't only that at the beginning of a trip the entire world is shiny and bright and possible, but also that we get to believe it again. Before any fractures show, before we feel like we are running out of time, before we make a bad choice. Before we realize that we are the reason something is going terribly wrong. In the beginning, we get to believe that, this time, we're going to get it exactly right.

When Griffin and I drove into Williamsburg for the first time—drove down its very sleepy Main Street, past the church steeple and the post office, all the Christmas trees still standing, light snow falling onto the remnants of a previous day's thick snowfall—I wasn't quite sure what moved me so much, why I felt so content. But I pulled out my camera and immediately started taking photographs. I had, over the years, driven down a hundred Main Streets made up of similar components. I could, in fact, think of many that were more picturesque. But there was something different this time. Something oddly specific. Like I had been there before. Or maybe like I knew I'd be there again. Seeing it for the thousandth time instead of the first. Something you'd only recognize one way—as a place you were supposed to be.

And I must have been wearing my enthusiasm on my face because Griffin lowered my camera and met my eyes. Gave me his biggest smile.

"Makes a good first impression, doesn't it?" he said.

I nodded. "It does," I said.

Griffin took a right off Main Street, and then another, until we were crawling into the outskirts of town: the picture-perfect Craftsman houses lined up like jewelry charms, shiny and bright against the snow. We drove farther out—the houses separating out from each other, space growing between them, farms starting to pop up. Then we took a final right onto Naples Road, and he slowed the car down.

There it was. A modest Craftsman, all by its lonesome. Griffin's house. My dream house. I don't mean that in any overly indulgent way—like it was the most special house I'd ever seen or the house I'd always longed for—I mean, quite literally, it was a house I'd seen in my dreams. Nighttime dreams, daytime ones. Same blue shutters and strong posts, a wooden porch complete with rocking chairs. Two windows peeking out from the second story, like eyes. A white brick chimney. Making me smile.

There was the wedding, of course. In a small chapel right

near the Las Vegas border, on our way across the country. It involved an ivory sundress, a pair of seventy-year-old witnesses, simple gold wedding bands, and a poem "Happiness" that Griffin read out loud to me. There was a very fun (and too-fast) car trip minimoon across the rest of the country together. There was all of that. But the two of us sitting in the car, on Naples Road— the world's smallest U-Haul trailing out behind us, carrying the pieces of my old life that I'd decided to bring (a few striped chairs, my file cabinets, my favorite photographs of Mila)—that was the moment. I was staring at this house I was sure I'd seen before— and that was the beginning of my new life, my new marriage.

I twirled my wedding ring around my finger. "So," I said, "This is where we live now?"

He nodded. "This is where we live now," he said. "You ready to head in?"

Before I could answer, Griffin shut off the car and walked around to open the passenger door. He opened the door for me and proceeded to pick me up in his arms, carrying me down the snowy sidewalk—pausing at the front door, preparing to carry me over the threshold, into the house.

I was laughing, a little uncomfortably, mostly because I felt embarrassed. I wasn't good at displays of romantic affection, especially traditional ones. I used to think that I found them corny. It would only occur to me later that it wasn't so much that I found them corny, but that I found them unfamiliar. But Griffin seemed determined to change that, moving us confidently in the direction of the front door, turning the knob while holding me, moving us both inside, onto the green hallway mat that read WELCOME.

"We're here," Griffin said, and kissed me.

Only someone else answered. "Hey there . . ."

A man's voice came from deep inside the house, and Griffin dropped me, bottom first, onto the welcome mat, right on top of the WELCOME.

I looked up, shocked. First at Griffin, who looked angry, then at the guy he was staring angrily at, who was casually standing in front of us, eating a Fudgsicle. He had a four-day shadow, his dark hair uncombed. But that couldn't hide how handsome he was, with piercing green eyes and a smile that matched Griffin's. There was a small child on either side of him—one with his own Fudgsicle, one holding what looked like a plastic yellow watering can. They were five-years-old, six at the oldest. And they were twins. Practically identical, very adorable redheaded twins.

"You scared the shit out of me," Griffin said.

"Will you watch your language for Christ's sake?" the guy said. "We have impressionable children here."

Griffin leaned down to pick me up off the floor. "You okay?" he asked. "Did I hurt you?"

"No . . ."

I shook my head, as Griffin lifted me up. I was more startled than anything else, looking up at him, looking over again at the two small boys. They smiled widely, seemingly enjoying all of this. They were beautiful little boys with that red hair and enormous green eyes. They looked quite a bit like the man I was assuming was their dad—same shape to their faces, those same green eyes. But their awesome red hair, that must have come from somewhere else.

"Aren't you guys going to hug your Uncle Griffin hello?" he said. Then he simultaneously patted the boys on their heads.

Uncle Griffin.

This was Jesse. Of course, it was Griffin's brother Jesse. Griffin hadn't had family photographs with him in Los Angeles, but it made perfect sense. He had told me that Jesse had little boys—had he told me that they were twins?—Sammy and Dexter, if I was remembering correctly. I knew they lived in Boston, which wasn't so far from western Massachusetts. Jesse was a graduate student working toward his PhD at MIT. And Jesse's wife—what had Griffin told me her name was?—owned a flower shop in Cambridge. That was what I knew. And now I knew this: behind those eyes, and that Fudgsicle, Jesse was looking a little crazed at the moment.

"They're having a silent contest right now," Jesse said, gently pushing both boys in Griffin's direction. "Go on, guys. No talking necessary."

The twins ran to Griffin, who scooped them up into his arms, holding both of them close—one hand cupped under each small body, his eyes still drilled into his brother.

I noticed it, right on the other side of Griffin and the boys, at the foot of the stairs: several enormous suitcases and piles of clothes. Sporting equipment. Children's toys. All of it partially unpacked and spilling up the stairway, spilling all the way down the upstairs hallway, which, from my angle at least, was a total and complete disaster: paintings falling from their hangers, carpet ripped up. And the distinct smell of grape juice, coming from somewhere that I wasn't sure I wanted to visit.

Griffin must have followed where my eyes went because he looked that way too, and then back at his brother.

"Jesse, how long have you been staying here?" Griffin asked.

Jesse shrugged. "Not long."

"How *not* long?"

"Not long," he answered. "Like five weeks."

"Five *weeks?*" I said.

It was the first thing I'd said. And Jesse turned to me—for the first time—as if just noticing I was there. Standing in front of him. After falling out of his brother's arms.

"Hey there," he said.

"Hey there," I repeated.

Then I gave him a small wave, more than a little surprised I had opened my mouth at all.

"How could you not have told me you were here?" Griffin said.

Jesse tuned back to his brother, offering up a shrug. "Didn't want to worry you," he said. "Seemed unnecessary."

Griffin put down the twins, who raced wordlessly up the stairs, fighting back their laughter, fighting hard not to tumble and trip over the massive amount of belongings covering the floor. I watched them go, my eyes shifting back to Jesse once they'd disappeared, a bedroom door slamming behind them. The only noise.

"What do the kids get for winning the silent contest?" I asked. "They seem incredibly committed."

"A hundred bucks," Jesse said.

"That's some prize," I said.

This made Jesse smile. "I believe it breeds a certain level of commitment," he said.

Griffin drilled his brother with a look. "Where's Cheryl, Jessie?"

"Cheryl kicked me out," Jesse said.

"She kicked you out?" he said.

Jesse nodded, his voice getting smaller. "Sammy hasn't put down Cheryl's watering can since. The kid even sleeps with it. That means he's traumatized, right? We've probably traumatized him. Dex seems to be handling it all a little better, but last night he took a hard swing at Sammy to try to get that can. So I can't really take that as a sign of progress."

Griffin just stared at his brother. "Cheryl kicked you out? Why would she do that?"

"Well, she needed to catch her breath for a minute," Jesse said. "That can happen."

"When, Jesse? When can that happen?"

"You know," he said, "when you find out your husband got someone else pregnant."

I looked at him in disbelief—*what did he just say?* As if reading my thought, Jesse nodded again.

"It's complicated," Jesse said.

I looked at Jesse for so long that someone might have wondered if I were thinking it was possible that he was going to take his words back, say something different instead. But maybe I was also looking at him for that long because I was scared to look any other way—to catch Griffin's eyes and see what he was or wasn't thinking about what his brother had just revealed.

But Griffin wasn't saying a word. The next several, I was guessing, were going to have to come from Jesse. Then they did. And they were for me.

"I'm sorry," he said. "Griffin's a little rude. I'm Jesse. Griffin's brother. Who are you?"

He held out his hand, which I imagined was sticky from the Fudgsicle. But I took it.

"Griffin's wife," I said.

"He's actually a genius, believe it or not," Griffin said. "Like a certified one. His IQ is off the charts and he skipped two grades in school when we were growing up. Got a full ride to MIT at sixteen years old. Though maybe that did more damage than good. . . ."

We were lying in bed—my first night in our bed—and I was staring at the ceiling, only a bedside light still on. I was blinking too quickly, trying not to give into the tight ball taking hold in my chest, trying not to focus on the little-person-size hole in the wall near our bedroom door—the result of a paintball fight gone awry. It was now covered with a bedsheet that was unequal to the task of keeping out the outside world.

Instead of focusing too hard on any of that, I tried to make out the designs on the ceiling overhead, still mostly visible in the soft light: the intricate and beautiful designs, interstitial numbers and words, stand-alone letters, an entire system I couldn't quite comprehend, right above my head. Griffin had just come to bed, after a longer conversation with Jesse, one I didn't partake in, one in which Jesse provided some details about this other woman—he knew her from graduate school—and fewer details about what he was going to do now.

Now Griffin was whispering. I knew why and I wasn't sure why. Jesse and the kids were in a bedroom across the hall, watching a movie—*Raiders of the Lost Ark,* I believed—the volume turned to high. They were laughing and shouting at the screen, shouting louder than the movie itself. Silent contest apparently over.

"I just wish that you hadn't gotten such a bad first impression of him," Griffin said.

"It wasn't so bad," I said. "Really . . ."

Then I cleared my throat because I wasn't sure what to say next. A bad first impression, though, seemed like the wrong terminology. Someone's mother being loud or eerily quiet was a bad first impression. Someone's childhood friend drinking too much wine and getting silly. But finding a married brother-in-law living in your new house with his young twin sons because he'd impregnated a woman who wasn't his wife? That seemed like something else.

Still, I tried to think of something supportive to say—something to get both of us out of our heads. But, the truth was, I was feeling judgmental of Jesse. And that wasn't the only problem. This was the first time since I'd met Griffin that I was aware there was something I didn't know how to say to him.

Griffin turned onto his side to face me, resting his hand on his elbow.

"They just don't have anywhere else to go right now," he said. "I mean, I guess they could go stay at my mother's in New York City, but Jesse hasn't really told her what's going on yet. He doesn't want to deal with her reaction and I can't say I exactly blame him for that."

"I get it," I said.

And I did. From what Griffin had told me about his mother. She was a geology professor at New York University. A fitting profession being that she was so steady for the family, filling the house with so much love. But while she was apparently incredibly loving, she was also incredibly emotional. Especially when it came to her sons. And high emotions right now wouldn't help anything.

"He just needs some time to sort this all out. And with the twins going to a kindergarten near here for now and Jesse feeling good about that . . ." Griffin said. "I don't know if I feel right asking them to leave right now."

"No." I shook my head, gaining some resolve. "No, of course not. I'd never ask you to do that. I'd never ask you to ask him to leave. He's your brother. And he needs you."

"But you're my wife," he said. "And so do you."

He wrapped his arm tightly around me, so I could hear that that mattered to him too.

"I'll be fine," I said. "I promise you."

"This is just such a bad time for all of this, you know? We just got here. We're trying to settle in. You're trying to get used to everything. It's just such a bad time. . . ."

I moved closer to him. "Griffin," I said, "I'm not sure there is ever a good time to move in with your brother because you got a woman pregnant. Really not sure that's ever making it on to a greeting card."

Griffin laughed, kissing me sweetly on the forehead. "You've got a point there," he said.

"We'll be fine," I said. "We'll just, you know, have to lock the door when we have sex."

"And make sure the sheet is secure," he said.

I smiled.

Then that was what he did.

I woke up the next morning disoriented and more than a little confused. It wasn't unlike when you take a nap in the afternoon and wake up in the evening, no daylight left to help you out, the scrambling starting in your mind: Why am I asleep right now? What day is it? Am I home?

Part of the reason for my confusion was that Griffin's bedroom was still so dark—middle-of- the-night dark—due to the brown, floor-length curtains that apparently could keep out all forms of light. It was probably not a bad system for a chef who often needed to sleep during weird hours. But as I started coming to, I didn't like not knowing what time it was, whether I had even made it through the night yet. Why Griffin was gone.

I flipped over onto my stomach, pushed a thick curtain out of the way, and peeked beyond it, out into the world. The winter sun was streaming in hard and fast. It was so strong, in fact, that it reminded me of a California morning. I put my hand on the windowpane, waiting for warmth to hit my palm, but it was ice-cold. Burning me. The little thermometer on the pane's edge weighing in a minute too late at a whopping six degrees.

I got out of bed, threw on sweatpants and an extra pair of socks, and headed downstairs to the kitchen, where I found Jesse and the twins at the kitchen table, having breakfast. Jesse was dressed in a wrinkled suit, working hard on tying a tie around his neck while the twins focused on eating their Eggo waffles. Or, rather, Dexter was focused on sticking his tongue through the circle he'd made in the middle of his waffle, and on spinning the waffle around his face. Sammy, meanwhile, was stuffing his waffle into the watering can. The maple syrup—or what was left of it—was in two puddles beneath their feet.

"Good morning," I said.

Jesse looked up and smiled at me in the doorway. "Hey there, sis-in-law," he said.

"Hey there," I said, still standing in place, somewhat awkwardly. My feet, even through the socks, were getting pretty cold on the wooden floor. So, while I was trying to stay still, I was also moving from one foot to another.

"You like coffee?" Jesse asked.

"Only the first four cups I have each day," I said. "The fifth starts to lose me."

"Then you're at the right place, come sit for a minute," he said. "We've got some great freaking coffee."

He pointed with his tie in the direction of the thin, silver thermos in the middle of the table. His proof.

I headed to the table, taking the empty seat next to him, as Jesse let his tie go for a second and reached over to screw open the thermos for me, pouring some coffee into the cuplike top, handing it over.

The steam was piping out the top and I breathed it in, cupping it in my hands and taking a long sip.

"Whoa," I said. "You weren't kidding. This coffee is good. Out of this world good, actually."

"You're not wrong. I have approximately three things I'm really good at and making coffee is one of them." He looked back down at his tie, tugging it into a knot, and then undoing it. "I brought my French press from home. It's about a thousand years old. That's part of the trick."

I smiled as I blew on the top, took another sip. "And why the silver thermos?" I asked. "Is that part too?"

"No, just good for carrying it into Boston," he said. "I have a meeting in Cambridge this afternoon."

I stopped midsip. "Oh, I thought . . ."

He put up his hand to stop me. "Please, with my current behavior, offering up the good coffee is the least I can do," he said. "It's also, unfortunately, at this particular moment, the most."

He gave me a sweet smile, his hand holding his lopsided tie, still completely undone.

"You need a hand with that?" I asked.

He shook his head. "I'll get it," he said. "Probably when it's already too late. But I'll get it."

"Sounds like a plan," I said.

He was looking back down at his tie, going for it again, as I drank the coffee.

"But I would enjoy if you'd entertain me with the story of how you and my big brother fell in love," he said. "I can't believe I didn't know anything about what was happening with you guys. In another world, I could be pretty pissed off about that."

I laughed. "It just happened so quickly," I said.

"'The only laws of matter are those that our minds must fabricate and the only laws of mind are fabricated for it by matter.'"

I looked at him, completely confused.

"James Clerk Maxwell. The guy who created classical electromagnetic theory," he said. "I like to think it's another way of saying great things tend to happen all at once."

I smiled. "I like that," I said. "A lot . . . Is that what you're in graduate school for?"

"In a way," he said. "An updated version. I'm working with a scientist named Jude Flemming, have you heard of her? I'm guessing not unless you're up on the world of optical physics."

"Not so much recently, no."

"Well, Dr. Flemming is amazing, inspirational really. She's only in her mid-forties and she already heads the department. Not to mention that she's considerably changing how we understand optical fields," he said.

"Those of you who understand it," I said.

"Exactly." He laughed. Then he pointed it in the direction of the counter. "By the way, Griffin left you a little love note over there. He didn't want to wake you, but he had to head over to the restaurant to meet a contractor. He left you directions in case you want to go by and say hello."

I nodded. "Great, but I thought he told me he wasn't heading over there until eleven or so," I said. "What time is it?"

"It's twelve forty-five."

"Twelve forty-five?" I asked. I was in total disbelief. In my life, the entirety of it to that point, I had never slept that late. In the entirety of my life, I had never slept anywhere close to that late: work starting at 6:00 A.M. most days, work supposed to have started *today* at 6:00 A.M., so I wouldn't be so late getting the latest column to Peter.

"It's those brown curtains, right?" he said. "They'll do you in if you're not careful."

"You're not kidding," I said.

"We got a late start too, and I'm now completely screwed for my meeting," he said. "Unless I go eighty miles per hour all the way there. Who am I kidding? Even if I go eighty all the way there."

"Who is your meeting with?" I asked.

"My faculty adviser," he said.

"Jude Flemming?"

"Jude Flemming," he said. "I need to ask her for an extension on my dissertation. I get a little nervous asking her for anything."

"I can understand that." I poured myself some more coffee. "How late are you getting the dissertation in?" I asked.

"You know, about nine years."

I stopped midpour.

"There are reasons," he said.

I nodded. "I'm sure," I said.

Then he stood up, his tie loose around his neck, and he began grabbing for several things at once: his keys, the mostly empty thermos, a shabby briefcase on the counter. "So you think you could take them?" he said.

I looked at him, confused. "Take who?"

"Sammy and Dex," he said. "To school. The afternoon part, at least. It's walking distance from here. And it would really help me out. They have an indoor peewee soccer league afterward that will keep them busy until after I'm back, but can you take them over there?"

"Me?" I said, turning to the twins, who were still busy with their waffles, not so much as looking in my direction. "But they don't know me, Jesse. Won't that be weird?"

Jesse turned toward them too. "Okay guys, this is your Aunt Annie." He patted the top of my head. "Tell her hello."

They turned to me, giving me a once-over, neither of them saying a word, neither offering a wave.

"Hi guys!" I smiled at Sammy who was holding on tight to his watering can. "I like your planter," I said.

Still, nothing.

"Okay, so, whichever of my big guys wants Annie to take them to school today *more* should tell her his name *loudest*, right now," he said. "Winner gets a hundred bucks."

Both boys raised their hands high. *"Me! Me!"* they screamed in a rising, vocal unison.

Then Dex waved his arms and screamed out, "I'm Dex! I'm Dex!" And Sammy held up his yellowing watering can and—using its spigot as a microphone—joined him with, "I'm Sammy! I'm Sammy!"

Jesse smiled down at me, his tie somehow magically tied. "There we go," he said. "One problem solved."

We must have been a sight on the way to school, the wind and snowfall kicking up: Sammy and Dexter on either side of me, wrapped in enormous winter coats entirely covering their little bodies (Sammy's watering can sticking out from beneath his), me in a light fleece unequal to the wind, all of us holding hands—shouting at the cars passing by, shouting at street signs, shouting at the sky.

Even with the hundred dollars on the table, the boys had seemed nervous and unhappy to see their father go, and, so, in an attempt to cheer them, I suggested playing a game of I Spy as we walked.

I wasn't sure if it was exactly age appropriate, but Jordan played it with Sasha and that seemed like endorsement enough for the time being. And the boys seemed to enjoy it. In the twenty or so minutes it took us to go from door to door—from the quiet outskirts of town to its slightly less quiet center—they spotted train tracks, an out-of-business ice-cream parlor, a broken bicycle, several snowmen, a closed-down fruit stand (with the sign SEE YA IN MAY!), a giraffe (or, rather, a statue of a giraffe in someone's yard), and dogs of several sizes (the people walking the dogs, the twins were far less interested in).

When we got closer to school, they also spotted the Williamsburg General Store, where I made the mistake of stopping. Because there, on the newspaper rack in front of the store, were copies of several national newspapers, including the *New York Times,* complete with a small advertisement for *The Unbowed.* The ad consisted of a photograph of a creepy playground at night, complete with a blurry image of a couple on the swings, so blurry you could almost miss them. But you couldn't miss what was on the bottom of the print, in bold black letters. His name: NICK CAMPBELL.

My heart clenched. My heart clenched just seeing his name, right in front of me, where I couldn't ignore it.

After Dexter "I spyed" the General Store, I was pretty close to adding, *Funny because I spy a ghost.*

But by the time we turned onto the elementary school's grounds, I'd pulled it back together, which was a good thing because, despite the school not being impressively large, it was impressively busy: a sizable group of kids finishing their afternoon recess, another group starting a basketball game, another playing boxball, wrapped up tightly in hats and gloves and winter coats. I spotted a teacher by the front door, clipboard in her heavily mittened hands, who pointed us to the kindergarten classroom on the far end of the floor.

As we made our way there, I could hear music coming from the classroom. I was happily surprised to peek through the open door and take in a bright and colorful classroom full of paintings and art, and the entire kindergarten class, twenty-plus kids, engaged in a massive game of freeze dance. To Bach.

I knocked softly and one of the two adults circling the massive bunch of dancing peanuts gave me a big smile. She hurried over to the door, her high ponytail bobbing behind her.

"Hi hi hi!" she said. "We were wondering when you guys were going to get here! Come on in, we're on the French Suites."

She heralded the twins inside, and, as they joined the musical fray, she slipped back through the doorway and joined me in the hallway.

"I'm Claire, Dexter and Sammy's teacher," she said.

Then she pointed to the other woman in the classroom, outfitted in an oversized UMass sweatshirt with matching sweatpants. "And that's Carolyn, the assistant teacher. She's a graduate student in early education over at the university. We have her two days a week. Sometimes three. Needless to say, they are much better days."

I smiled. "I can imagine," I said. "I'm Annie. I'm the twins' . . . well, I guess I'm their aunt."

The words felt a little weird coming out of my mouth, but it was also the simplest explanation, or so I thought.

Except that Claire crossed her arms over her chest, a grin taking over her face. "I didn't know Cheryl had a sister!" she said. "It is *fantastic* to meet you. I know she and Jesse are in a bit of a hard place at the moment, but she's been checking in with me regularly. She's a strong lady, your sister. . . ."

I shook my head, intending to correct her, and quickly. "No, I'm actually not related to—"

But, before I could finish, there was a loud bang from inside the classroom. We turned to see Sammy and Dex, still in their long winter coats—standing on either side of the boom box— now on its back on the floor.

"Oh boy," she said. "That's my cue. It's really nice to meet you, Annie. I hope to see you soon."

"I'd like that," I said.

She started to head in, but then turned back, something occurring to her.

"Actually, you know what? Is the end of next week too soon?"

"Excuse me?" I said.

"Well, the kids have a class trip to the Children's Museum. The science and nature museum in Hartford?" She shook her head, as if already imagining the chaos of that. "Anyway, it's looking like we're a mother short for the excursion. And could definitely use the extra pair of hands. Aunts' hands count. Would you be willing to join in? Are you still going to be in town then?"

"I'm supposed to be, but I really never know my work schedule for sure. I'm a travel writer and I'm definitely heading back out on the road soon. I've actually never been on a break this long, but I just got married and . . ."

"Great!" she said. "Then it's settled! That's really great. Thank you! And if you have a minute on your way out, you should head down the back stairs and check out the breezeway. The holiday art show is still up. Our art teacher, Ms. Henry, is beyond incredible. And the twins did a painting of a purple Christmas tree. It rocks!"

I laughed. "I'm sure it does."

"Go see for yourself." Then she pointed at my fleece as she walked back inside. "And if you're sticking around, you need a real coat or you'll get a bad cold. And good luck getting rid of it before spring."

"Thanks for the advice."

"Anytime."

The door flew shut and I was left in the quiet hallway. I stared at the closed door for just a second—watched through the small window as she scrambled to right the boom box and get the kids dancing again. Then I headed the way she told me, down the staircase, toward the open breezeway, partly because I wanted to see the purple Christmas tree and partly because I wasn't so anxious to head back outside in my too-light fleece.

I was glad I did. As soon as I stepped onto the breezeway, I saw how right Claire was. A truly great display of paintings and collages and charcoal drawings was taped over the windows. I was captivated, walking slowly down the hall, checking out the artwork of each grade: snowmen and reindeer, bright scenes of stick-people Thanksgiving dinners. There was also a beautiful drawing of several pears among the second-graders' lot. (I wasn't sure what pears had to do with the holidays, but it was beautiful nevertheless.)

I was staring so hard at the pears that it took me a minute to realize I wasn't in the breezeway alone. There was another woman, who had made her way from the other end, trailing a metal dolly behind her. She was diminutive in a tea-length turtleneck dress and a beautiful, bright orange scarf, her long blond hair falling down her back. She was reaching high above her head to remove one of the paintings from its perch.

Even on her tiptoes, she was struggling to reach both corners at once, and was looking less than steady. So I walked over and reached for the upper left-hand corner, and the two of us pulled off the painting together.

"Oh, thank you for that!" she said, giving me a large smile as she rolled up the brown paper painting and gently placed it onto her dolly. "One down. A thousand to go."

"Seems like I got here just in the nick of time," I said.

She nodded, tilting her head to the side, and I couldn't help but notice that up close she was even more striking, with birdlike features, high cheekbones, dark eyelashes.

"Are you looking for anything in particular?" she asked.

"A purple Christmas tree, I believe."

"Ah . . ." Her smile got bigger as she pointed in the direction of several paintings a little farther down the breezeway, a forest of purple Christmas trees, grouped together under the sign KIN-DERGARTEN.

"I take it you know one of Claire's students?" she said.

"Two, actually."

"I do the best I can with them, but, this year, I got the kinder-garteners in to see me twenty-four hours after they were shown *Barney's Great Adventure*. What can I say?"

I laughed. "So you must be the incredible art teacher that Claire was just telling me about?"

"Art teacher, home ec teacher, currently going crazy teacher," she said, pushing her hair behind her ears. "But I'll gladly take Claire's description in place of that. And who are you?"

"Annie," I said. "Annie Adams. I just moved to town."

"Welcome!" she said. "I had a couple of clues that you're not from here, actually. You know, in addition to my having lived here my entire life, and the not-knowing-you part."

"What were those?"

She pointed at my Converse sneakers, and then at my fleece. "You can get pretty sick dressed like that," she said.

"I'm getting that idea," I said. "I recently got married and my husband's from here. Grew up here, actually. But, except for a work trip to the Berkshires last summer, I haven't spent any time in the area to speak of. So I guess I'm still figuring out what it's going to be like."

"Cold."

"And pretty," I said, hopefully.

"And cold."

Then she reached for another painting, started to pull at it. It had a blue ribbon underneath it. First prize written in gold on the front. Which was when I noticed every one of the paint-ings had a blue ribbon underneath it. First prize gold on all of them.

She shrugged. "There *was* supposed to be one winner, but I'm not a big one for competition," she said. "So I made it a two hundred–way tie."

"Sounds like a good solution," I said.

"It became less of one when all of the kids began asking me which one of them won the most." She shook her head in disbelief. "What are you going to do?"

Then, as she deposited another drawing on the dolly, I looked at the long wall, completely covered with artwork.

"You know what? I'm not in any rush. Can I give you a hand with some of these?"

She shined her smile at me, happily. "Really? You sure that you wouldn't mind?" she said. "I was going to ask the janitor to give me a hand, then I remembered we don't have one."

I laughed, reaching for the painting in front of me—of two stick figures hitting turkey drumsticks—gently pulling at the tape on the corners.

"It'd be my pleasure to help out."

She took her scarf off her neck, handed it over. "Well, please wear this while you do. I made it myself, lots of wool."

"It's so soft," I said, wrapping the scarf around my neck and instantly feeling better, the cool starting to seep out of me.

"Excellent, because I cannot look at you all exposed like that," she said. "And I'll give you some more lessons in finding warmth in Williamsburg while we work."

"Don't I just get more clothing?" I asked.

She sighed. "If only it were that simple."

I smiled, looking toward the next group of paintings and realizing we were coming up on the series of purple Christmas trees. And then I was right in front of it: the double tree bearing the names SaMMMMMy and DeXXXXX. Written just like that. Sadly, they weren't exactly good trees—even forgetting the purple. One could confuse them with flagpoles instead. Or pretzels.

I ran my fingers over the tree anyway, over the letters of their names. "These are them," I said.

"Them who?"

"My nephews," I said. "Sammy and Dexter Putney . . ."

"Sammy and Dexter?" she asked.

And then she went white. She went so white, right in front of my eyes, that suddenly I understood the expression "seeing a ghost." All of a sudden, I could see one.

She stared at me for a long minute. "So are you related to Jesse's wife or something?" she said. "You must be related to Cheryl, right? She has a stepsister, I think. Or maybe you're just a good friend of the family. The kind of friend they call aunt . . ."

But she started talking very low. She started talking very low, and in the voice of someone who already had a question's unfortunate answer.

"No, I'm actually married to Jesse's brother, Griffin," I said. "Just recently, though."

The air started to close out of the room. I didn't know how— or why—but I could feel it condensing around us.

"How just recently?"

"We met in Los Angeles while he was filling in at a restaurant near where I live. Or where I lived, I guess."

I gave her a smile, but she wasn't having it. So I kept talking.

"The whole thing happened really fast, actually . . ." I said. "I probably shouldn't tell you how fast or you'll get the wrong impression about me. I've never done anything like this before. Impulsive like this, before." I felt myself blushing a little. "And I've always hated people who say things like, 'When you know, you know.' I've never just known about anything else. Not even a pair of socks."

She was staring at me, as if with a growing level of concern that I might be a lunatic.

"Well, maybe there was one pair of socks at some point. For the gym or something . . ."

Nothing. She said nothing. I was still talking, telling her more than she could possibly want to know, more than anyone could.

But I couldn't seem to stop. I couldn't seem to stop trying to do something to bring her color back.

Then I noticed it on the inside of her wrist—the other half of Griffin's tattoo. The other half of the anchor. The right half. The sharper one.

"Oh my gosh, wait. You're Gia?"

She nodded. "I'm Gia."

"Griffin told me about you! I guess not your last name, though," I said. "But he told me about the tattoo. I love it. I mean, I love the tattoo. But I also love that you guys did that together."

I was still smiling. This is the worst part: I was still smiling when I said this. I didn't quite know yet that I shouldn't be. Then Gia, my former new friend, walked away from me. She turned and walked away from me, fast.

And I got my first idea.

13

Something else I discovered from writing "Checking Out," something that should not be underrated, is the joy people feel when they get to pretend to be someone else for a while. When you travel, you can become anyone. No one knows you. No one is telling you who—based on your history, or their ideas about your history—they've decided you are. When you travel, everything is unfamiliar and possible again. Like with a brand-new job or a brand-new partner. Like with a first kiss. For a short, perfect while, you get to see yourself—you get to experience yourself—as new. Until the inevitable (and inevitability surprising) reminder: you are still you.

I walked through town in a fog, the directions to Griffin's restaurant in my fleece jacket's pocket, taking too many wrong turns anyway. Then I found a small, barnlike structure—slightly hidden from Main Street, unless you knew to look for it—with an amazing red chimney, scaffolding surrounding it, a sign (matching the chimney's red) without a name on it yet, still resting on the ground by the front door, still waiting to be raised.

I walked inside—the Rolling Stones' *Exile on Main Street*

blasting out its glory from a floor-side stereo—to find the place midconstruction, working toward its own glory: unfinished floors and markings on the walls, electrical wires coming from the ceiling. A large, rectangular hole in the far wall that I imagined was going to be the bar area. A cool, metal chandelier waiting to be raised above it, Griffin touching its top as he talked to several men.

When he looked up and saw me standing there, he gave me a big smile and headed my way.

"You're here," he said.

"I'm here."

He pulled me into the unoccupied corner, giving me a long kiss.

"Is it crazy that I missed you today?" He pulled back, taking a look at me. Then he began running his hands over my cheeks. "And why are you so cold? You can't be dressing like that. You're going to get pneumonia."

"I wish everyone would stop pointing that out. And I wish it would stop getting worse."

He looked at me, confused. "Getting worse?"

"The length of my hospital stay."

He started laughing, which quickly turned into a cough and just as quickly turned scary, leaving me completely unsure what to do as he braced himself on his knees, trying and failing to catch his breath. He managed to reach for the inhaler in his pocket, putting it to his lips and taking a long, deep puff. His breath, the coughs, finally starting to slow.

"Are you okay?" I asked.

He nodded, his voice returning. "Fine," he said. "It sounds a lot worse than it actually is."

He was still resting on his knees, though.

"It's all the dust in here," he said. "It got right into my lungs. Brutal."

"Maybe it's not such a good idea to be around it?" I said.

"Definitely not," he said.

But he was standing up again and smiling as he said it. Only then did I realize how fast my heart was beating.

"Don't worry," he said. "It sounds worse than it is."

"You said that already. . . ."

"So I guess it must be true."

He took my hand, giving it a firm squeeze, then a second one as if to say, *I'm fine, really.*

I squeezed back, *I'm glad.*

Then he motioned toward the ceiling and all around himself, proudly. "So?" he said. "I know it's just the bones of the place still, but what do you think? What do you think of our so-far-unnamed endeavor?"

I looked at Griffin for another second and then looked around, trying to envision the restaurant—what it would be—beneath the construction. The bones were already hinting at how great it was going to look: wide-open beams and rafters, rustic tables of different sizes and a hearth oven, lanterns everywhere. And, of course, that large fireplace leading to the red top.

"I think it's going to be amazing," I said. "Really amazing."

He gave me a big smile. "The Stones are seeping into the walls," he said. "Giving the room some flavor."

"Maybe you should call the restaurant the Stones, then?"

"I'm not so sure about that."

"How about Annie's Place then? Or just . . . Annie's? Everyone likes a place called Annie's. I think both have a certain ring to them."

I smiled so he'd know I was mostly kidding. In response, he wrapped his arms around me.

"I'll put those in the file for sure," he said, bending down and kissing the side of my face, holding there. "And how has your day been going? I was getting a little worried. I called the house a few times and you didn't pick up."

"I ended up bringing the twins to school."

I thought I felt it then, just the softest tension—his lips

against my cheek starting to release. But then, almost as quickly, he was back with me, lips pressing against my skin.

"That was nice of you."

"It wasn't a big deal," I said. "Jesse needed to get into Boston for a meeting with his dissertation adviser."

"It was a big deal," he said. "Aren't you on deadline for your latest 'Checking Out'?"

Another reminder that I was on deadline—Peter anxiously reminding me himself via phone and e-mail, at increasingly frequent intervals. A looming deadline not only to turn in the new column, but to make a decision as to where I wanted to travel next. The answer no closer to coming to me.

But I just smiled and shrugged. "It was kind of fun, actually," I said. "I saw a little of the town. Got to hang with the twins, and see their school. Plus, I met Gia."

This time I knew I wasn't imagining his tension.

"You met Gia?" he said.

I nodded. "In the breezeway. We ended up talking for a little while and she seemed lovely to me. A little like she could give Martha Stewart a run for her money, but I actually thought maybe I made a first friend here. I know that sounds like I'm in high school, but it felt like I knew her or something. She just seemed . . . lovely to me."

"You mentioned . . ."

"Is she not?"

"No," he said. "She is. She's lovely."

I looked up, met his eyes. "Right, so I'm trying to figure out how I offended her. All I know is she walked away from me quickly after I told her we had gotten married. Why would she care about that? You dated in *high school*."

Griffin closed his eyes, slightly shaking his head. "Shit," he said.

"What? She can't still be into you after all this time. That's crazy. I mean, I'll never get over you, but . . ."

Griffin opened his eyes, looking at me, not smiling at my joke. Or, for that matter, at me.

"Annie," he said, "I never said that Gia was just my high school girlfriend. I never said that to you."

"What do you mean? Yes, you did."

I racked my brain for the information I was holding on to, until I recalled the conversation I'd been thinking of, the one in which he mentioned her: the two of us sitting next to each other at the hotel bar, my fingers on his half of the tattoo, Griffin talking about the night he got it.

"You said you got that tattoo at eighteen, right?"

He nodded. "Right."

Then I started to get it, what apparently I'd missed. "You and Gia were together longer than that?" I said.

He nodded again. "Right."

"How much longer than that?" I said.

He looked behind himself toward the workers, a few of whom were looking our way, waiting for him. "Maybe we should go outside for a minute. Let's go outside and have a real discussion about this."

"How much longer, Griffin?"

He looked right at me, looked right into my eyes. "Thirteen years," he said.

"Thirteen *years?*"

I was dumbstruck. I'd always hated that expression—still hate it—someone being dumbstruck. And, yet, in writing a travel column, one would be surprised how many times Peter thought it was appropriate for me to be so: dumbstruck at the Burj Al Arab hotel, dumbstruck at the Big Ben. Dumbstruck at the Milan Duomo. I never was—or I never wrote that I was, at least. But standing in front of my new husband and learning he had been with someone before me for close to *a decade and a half,* I wasn't sure how else to articulate the feeling. No other word seemed to do it.

"Look, it's all a little complicated," he said. "And I really didn't want to burden you with it, for all the reasons I told you in California. I don't think it's helpful in a new relationship to get into it all too much."

"How about getting into it just a little? Just a little might have been good," I said. "And what do you know about new relationships anyway? You've had the same girlfriend since you were a fetus."

He ignored me, which was probably wise right then.

"I can't believe you were with someone so long," I said. "I can't believe you were with someone *else* for that long."

I felt it bubbling up inside of me, jealousy, and something like a revelation: if time were at least part of the measure of real love—how long it would take, how long it would have to take—for us to know each other the way we'd known the people who came before.

"The important part is that we were broken up well before you and I got together," he said. "We broke up before I even left for Los Angeles."

"How long before, Griffin?" I asked. "Six months?"

"Closer to nine," he said.

"Oh, well, then . . ."

"I was going to get into the details, but I wanted to speak to Gia first. I thought it'd ease things once I knew where she was with everything. I was hoping that by my leaving town for a while, it would put our separation in a better place for her. That she would understand, as hard as it was, that going our own ways was really for the best. For both of us."

"So you left her?"

"I did."

"Why?"

He looked pained. "Annie, it was over with Gia for a long time before it was over," he said. "I can't explain it exactly. I couldn't do it anymore, if that makes any sense. It certainly didn't to her. . . ."

I nodded. Because it did make sense—at least the part about

Gia's not understanding. That's the brutality of a breakup, isn't it? The people leaving think they did everything possible, the people left behind think what is possible hasn't even been tested yet.

"Look, we can talk about this more. We can go into all of it tonight, if that will help. But you need to believe that. You need to believe we were done before I met you. I should have been more forthcoming about how long our history was. But it really is history. I think you know that's true."

I did know that—could feel it, actually—which was when a bit of the confusion and jealousy subsided, and I heard the first part of what he said. And I began to process it.

"Wait a minute," I said. "But she knew, right? She knew from you? That you're married now?"

He didn't answer.

"You didn't tell her?"

He shook his head. "I tried a hundred times to talk to her. But she wouldn't take my calls. She didn't respond to my e-mails that I had news for her and we needed to talk. And it felt cruel to spell it out over e-mail. I thought it would be kinder to wait until I was back, to bite the bullet and tell her in person."

"So you're telling me that I'm the one who informed your girlfriend of thirteen years that you married someone else less than a year after the two of you broke up?"

I shook my head and looked down. Then I saw it, what I was still wearing around my neck. "And I stole her scarf!"

"Annie, come on . . ."

I headed out to the street, Griffin following close behind. I didn't know where I wanted to go, maybe just somewhere that this conversation could start over again. But then I turned back to look at him. He looked so upset. He looked so upset that it stopped me.

I looked at him. "I'm a terrible person," I said.

"Why would you say that?"

I didn't know exactly how to answer him. I didn't know how to explain that as disorienting as his revelations were, something was bothering me even more. It almost killed me. It almost killed me that Nick had *maybe* found someone else so quickly. It almost killed me wondering why he was drawn to someone who seemed so different than me—that seemed so able to fill the holes for him that I couldn't. And now, without even knowing it, I'd become this other woman to someone else. I had become this other woman to her, and moved right into her hometown without any warning. Not to mention that, on top of the rest of it, I was being kept warm by her homemade orange scarf.

Then it occurred to me. "How could that not be the worst thing?" I asked.

He looked at me, confused.

"That you were with her for thirteen years? How could that not be the worst thing?" I said. "Or the best?"

He nodded.

"It was close," he said.

14

I got back to the house after dark. I'd left Griffin at the restaurant to finish up for the day, took the car, and went to find myself a coat. I felt like I was in no position to wrap my head around all the new information that seemed to be insistently coming at me—from Jesse, from Griffin, from *Gia*—but a new, warmer coat: that I could handle. But as I drove though Williamsburg's quiet streets—incredibly quiet, it seemed, only a handful of people outside—the only clothing store I could find was a small vintage shop, the lights already dimmed, looking mostly closed.

The saleswoman—sales teenager, more accurately—gave me a crazy look when I even walked inside. Or I thought she was giving me a crazy look, at least, but it was a little hard to make out her expression beneath her enormous, purple hat. Matching purple glasses.

"Hi there," I said.

She nodded.

"It's sleepy out there today, isn't it?" I said.

"Well, it's after five," she said.

"Right, of course . . ." I said. Then I shook my head, confused. "Wait, what do you mean that it's after five?"

She shrugged. "It's the rule of five."

For a minute I thought she too knew there was a new person in town (me) and was making a joke at the new girl's expense. But then, when I started to giggle—trying to be a good sport—she didn't join in.

"Why's that so funny? It's just the *rule.*"

She rolled her eyes, as if in complete disbelief that this didn't clear up the entire situation for me.

"After five P.M., from November through March, you rarely see more than five people on the streets around here."

"That's a little like people walking around in Los Angeles, any time of the year," I said.

I started to laugh. She, on the other hand, wasn't at all amused. "Can I help you with something?" she said.

"Would you mind just pointing me in the direction of the winter coats?"

She nodded toward the back of the small store, and the only two coats she had left: a floor-length black wool coat with red and green sequined rhinestone hearts plastered all over it. In a small. And the same coat in an extra large.

When I walked into the house a little while later—in the cruel and enormous extra large version—I found Jesse at the kitchen table, still dressed in his suit. He was making his way through two six-packs of beer, and eating Chinese food straight from the array of take-out containers littering the table.

"Nice coat, lady!" he said.

I sat down across from him. "Not a good moment to start with me about it," I said.

"Who's starting with you? It's badass." It took me only half a second to see that he was serious. "Completely badass."

Then he held a container in my direction. "Shrimp lo mein?"

I shook my head. "No thanks, I'm not hungry."

"You sure?"

I looked in the container, the shiny, colorful noodles staring back at me.

"You're right, I am." I sighed. "I'm always hungry, apparently, even when I'm totally depressed. Which is why between the small coat and the extra-large one there wasn't much of a contest."

Jesse gave me a confused look. "I'm just going to pretend I followed that," he said.

"Probably for the best," I said.

Then he handed over the lo mein, plus a packet of hot mustard sauce to go with it. As I poured the sauce over the noodles, he started in on a container marked PEKING BEEF AND BROCCOLI, taking an impressively large bite.

"So why are you depressed?" he asked, his mouth full.

I paused before answering. "I met Gia."

His eyes got wide. "Gia Henry?"

"Is there more than one?" I asked.

Then his eyes got wider as I could see him making the connections: kids to school, school to Gia, Gia to heart-sequined coat.

"Man," he said. "That's kind of my fault, isn't it?"

I shrugged. "Griffin was the one who dated someone else for *thirteen years* and didn't find it necessary to give me a heads-up about the fact that it just ended. Or that she still lives around the corner."

"Don't be mad at him about that. Everyone still lives around the corner. That's the thing about Williamsburg. No one leaves. Or they don't get too far. We're all one dysfunctional family."

"That's so not comforting."

He smiled. "Well, take comfort in the fact that she's more like three corners away, actually."

I looked up at him.

"You have to walk over to North Farms Road. Then Mountain Street . . ." He was motioning with his fingers, marking the direction you needed to go. To get to her. "Then over the bridge to High!"

The noodles were still in my mouth—greasy-hot, slippery— and it was all I could do to keep chewing.

"She used to live here? In this house?" I said.

"Maybe?" he said.

How could that surprise me? Thirteen years, where else would they be, but under the same roof? *My* roof. Hers first.

Jesse pushed a beer in my direction. I reached for it, opening the top.

"This is turning into a great day," I said.

"Ah, what are you so freaked about, anyway?" he shook his head. "You guys are completely different."

"That's what I'm so freaked-out about," I said. "I know I just met her, but, on the surface at least, she seems more Griffin's match than me."

He waved his hand away. "What does the surface tell you?" he said. "Besides, that was a loyalty thing. Not a love thing."

I picked up the beer, and took a long swig. Then I took another. "Meaning what, exactly?" I said.

"Meaning, there are different reasons that people stay with someone. Over time, there are different reasons." He picked the noodles back up. "You can tell when you're in the presence of true love and when you're in the presence of something closer to friendship."

"And with them it was closer to friendship?" I said.

"Well, not first. At first they were crazy about each other. . . ."

He started laughing, recalling an apparently *hilarious* memory involving how crazy my husband was for his ex-girlfriend. I must have given him some look because he stopped laughing, his eyes getting wide, nervous, as he tried to change the direction we were going.

"The point is that yes, sure, they loved each other when they were young, but something shifted," he said. "They had become each other's family, but they didn't have that initial draw anymore. That draw that, you know, makes you feel certain about someone."

"Who gets to have that all the time? Who in the history of the world has ever gotten to have that forever?"

He held the noodles to his mouth, thinking about it. "Joanne Woodward and Paul Newman . . . and probably someone else."

I shook my head, unable to stop myself from laughing. But even if it could have made me feel better (because he clearly wouldn't have said the whole thing about love and loyalty if he didn't think his brother and I fell on the love side of the boat), it actually made me feel something else more acutely. It made me feel defensive. Defensive for a girl with beautiful blond hair whom I'd just met for the first time. Defensive for myself too. And for all of us who gave years of ourselves—who gave the best pieces of ourselves—to someone who ultimately decided they weren't certain enough to fight for us.

"I think it's more complicated than that," I said.

Jesse shrugged. "Okay."

"I think, or I used to think at least, that real love comes over time, once that initial draw you're talking about takes on a different form. When you get to understand there is something more concrete between you," I said. "Something that is worth preserving . . ."

He tilted his head, looking at me confused. "And how's that different than what I just said?"

I shook my head. "I don't know," I said. "I'm starting to doubt I have any idea about what makes love work."

"Comforting, coming from my brother's wife."

I gave him a smile, trying to lighten the mood. But I was also thinking about what Jordan said, Jordan whom I'd been trying to avoid calling back, Jordan whom I'd been trying to avoid.

Sending her short e-mails, ignoring her hostile ones. What had she said that day? *If too much time goes by, men can forget what they have. How much they still want exactly what they have . . .*

Is the switch from love to something closer to loyalty really just another name for that very moment—that very challenge—and the inability to meet it? Was that just an excuse for Jesse to do what he did to his wife? How about Nick? How about my new husband?

And what did that say about what I was doing here?

I felt unready to address those questions, especially the last one, and the addendum to the last one, which had started circling around me: What exactly *was* I going to do here?

I pulled my coat tighter around me, the inside of the rhinestone hearts scratching at my arms.

"So how did it go today, anyway?" I asked, moving us into easier territory. "With your dissertation adviser?"

"Not so good," he said.

"No extension granted?"

He shook his head, picking up an egg roll. "Nope," he said.

"Just like that?"

"Just like that. I have eight weeks. Period. Eight weeks before I'm in front of a committee I couldn't be ready for in thirty weeks. But what can I do? Jude doesn't have much sympathy for my personal predicament."

"Jude knows?"

He nodded. "Jude knows."

This surprised me and made me wonder if he had misunderstood my question.

"No, what I mean is . . . you're saying that she knows what's going on with you? In terms of your personal life?" I asked. "She knows that you got a woman pregnant? Someone who isn't your wife?"

"You would assume so," he said, popping the entire egg roll into his mouth, starting to chew. "Considering it was Jude that I got pregnant."

I didn't know what to say. In my imagination it had been a graduate student or even an undergraduate student that Jesse had impregnated—a twenty-two-year-old who made him feel young and admired. Who made him new. Who confused being careless with carefree, and got herself involved with a married father of two. But this was shaping up to be something else, something with its own set of complications. Something that might involve optical fields.

I put my hand up to stop him from telling me anymore. "You know what? I'm sorry to hear you didn't get an extension. I really am. But I can't exactly deal with this right now," I said.

"Yeah . . ." He nodded. "That's what she said too."

Then, Jesse looked back up at me, something occurring to him.

"Your editor called, by the way, right when I was walking in the door. Some British dude. I think he said his name was Peter W. Shepherd?" Jesse offered up his name in a British accent.

I nodded. "That would be him."

"He sounded a little uptight."

"He is a little uptight."

"He also wasn't particularly happy," he said. "He said something about giving up on trying your cell phone now that you live in the boondocks. I wanted to say, *Dude, this is western Massachusetts, not the foothills of Tennessee.* But he'd probably have been like, *There's a difference?* So it's probably good I kept quiet."

"Probably."

"Either way," he said, "I hate to be the messenger on this one, but in case you aren't in the mood for any other surprises today, he did say you have to call him back as soon as possible. Those were his exact words. Apparently he has some bad news to report."

I pulled my coat tighter around me, unable to feel the hearts anymore, unable to let myself feel another bad thing.

"Of course he does," I said.

15
· · · · · · · · · · · · · · · · · ·

I n the entirety of my time writing "Checking Out," I had been to Peter's midtown Manhattan office only a handful of times. I couldn't begin to count the number of phone calls between us—Peter becoming a free-floating voice of calm, his sweet face largely one I'd drawn onto him in my mind. This was only one of the reasons it was so disconcerting sitting across from him— his sleek, modern desk between us—a black-and-white photograph of his beloved Steinbeck gracing the wall above his head. He looked like an alternative version of himself—less sweet, more reserved—with a rather large mole on the tip of his nose. I couldn't stop asking myself, how had I not noticed it before? And why was it all I could see now?

It had been five days since his phone call had come in. Five days since Peter had said that we needed to talk in person. So there I was in my black sheath dress and black blazer, my hair in a severe bun—looking more than a little like I was going to a funeral. Waiting for him to have at it, whatever *it* was.

"My love, you know that joke where the doctor tells his patient that he has good news and bad news?"

Apparently *it* was a punch line.

"I don't think so. . . ."

"Well," Peter said, "the joke goes that a doctor walks into an exam room and tells the patient he has good news and bad news and asks the patient which he wants to hear first. The patient picks the bad news. The doctor grimly tells him he has only a few months to live and needs to get his affairs in order. At which point, the saddened patient looks up and questions the doctor, 'What is the good news?' The doctor smiles and says, 'This morning, I had my best golf game in years.'"

I offered a small, conciliatory smile. "That's funny, Peter."

Peter shook his head, laughing. "Isn't it?" he said. Then he got serious. "So which would you like to hear first, my love, the good news or the bad news? It's your choice."

"Am I supposed to say the bad news?" I asked.

"That sounds right," he said. "And the bad news is that I'm being forced out of my position on the paper by the new editor in chief, Caleb Beckett the Second, who, in addition to having *no* journalism experience whatsoever, also happens to be quite an impressive postadolescent prick."

"I'm not following," I said, remembering our conversation from a few months ago, when the paper first changed hands. "Didn't you say that you liked the new publisher? That he was a gentleman of the oldest order?"

"I did. He is. But that's Caleb Beckett the *First*. This is Caleb Beckett Number *Two*. His son. And it's his son who he just made the editor in chief, and who he has given the latitude to do whatever he wants here in order to turn the paper into his darling. Except maybe . . . rent a car."

I tilted my head, trying to understand.

"The boy is twenty-four," he said.

I nodded. "Got it."

"Fine, he's closer to your age, but he may as well be a child, the way he is trying to do things. Australians . . ."

"Peter, what am I missing here?"

"Caleb's bringing in all these bloody television people to run the enterprise. Former classmates of his from Yale, who don't even read newspapers. They read the Internet. On their silly, electronic phones."

"I'm so sorry, Peter. I'm so sorry. You are an *incredible* editor. They are beyond lucky to have you," I said. "And believe me when I tell you, I am less than excited to work for someone like that."

"Well, that's when we get to the bad of the bad news," he said. "It's not going to be your option."

"What do you mean?"

"When your contract's up next month, they have decided they're not going to renew."

I looked at him, shocked. "They're canceling 'Checking Out'?"

He nodded. "They are, love. They're, in fact . . . checking out."

I gave him a look.

"Not a good joke?" he asked, sincerely surprised.

I shook my head, trying to understand. "But you said they were so happy with me. That I was a driver for advertisers, the bedrock of the travel section, that the column was one hundred percent safe."

"It turns out one hundred percent is a very tricky number."

I stared down at his desk. Had I just lost my job? After all this time? It seemed impossible—impossible without any warning signs. There was supposed to be safety in numbers, wasn't there? And I had at least some numbers on my side: columns, years, readers. None of those things had disappeared. All of those things were supposedly growing.

Then I started to wonder if maybe they were there, and I had missed them: the warning signs. Maybe I just hadn't been

looking closely enough to see them. Maybe I had been looking in the wrong place entirely, so I could pretend they weren't
there, so I didn't have to see what they were trying to tell me.

"They want to go big with the travel section," he said. "Create
international appeal. Everything has to be a platform. Complete
with a possible movie tie-in and a happy meal. That's the only
thing that will sell newspapers these days. Do you follow what
I'm saying?"

"Do *you* follow what you're saying?" I asked.

"Maybe we should be looking at the bright side," Peter said.
"You haven't been focused on the column in a while. Not the
way you used to be. Maybe it's a good time to move on."

He kept talking, though at some point I stopped listening.
I just sat there trying to take it in. It was over. "Checking Out"
was over. The one thing in my adult life I had been able to count
on. The one way I could feel free.

Finally, I looked back up at Peter.

"And what's the good news?" I said.

"The good news?" He started to beam. "Well, earlier this
week, I sold my novel to a brilliant young editor at a certain pub-
lishing house right down the road," he said. "It will be coming to
a bookstore near you this time next year."

I smiled, my heart opening a little. "That's great, Peter," I
said. "That's really great."

"The editor says that she sees the novel more in the vein
of Jack London than John Steinbeck, though. Can you believe
that? I guess, in the end, we really can't control these things."

"I guess not."

Then I forced a bigger smile, and looked him right in the eye,
trying to hold back my tears.

Peter reached across the table, taking my hand. "Don't be so
sad, my love," he said. "This is a blessing in disguise. There are a

million writing opportunities in Los Angeles. They have one of
the best travel magazines in the country, there's the L.A. *Times*
there. *LA Weekly* is doing some interesting things. . . ."

My heart clenched, started filling up my chest. "I live in
western Massachusetts now, remember?"

"That's a permanent thing?" he said, genuinely surprised.

"Peter . . ."

"So, that's not the end of the world. I have several contacts
in Williamstown for you. They have some wonderful writing
opportunities, I'm *sure*, related to theater and art."

"I live in Williams*burg*."

"Right," he said. "Probably less there."

It hit me all over again. If I'd still lived in Los Angeles, this
would be scary. But in California I had contacts, potential for
moving forward. Finding other opportunities. Where I was now,
I had just about none.

"Can I ask you something?" I said.

"Anything, my love."

"You said I haven't been focused in a while? On work. Haven't
my columns been good?"

"Sure, they've been good," he said. "But it's different recently."

"Define different."

"'Partly or totally unlike in nature, form, or quality,'" he said.
"'Dissmiliar. Divergent' . . ."

I gave him a look. "In regards to me."

"My love, you could probably write your fifteen hundred
words in your sleep by now. You could visit new cities, and find
their glory, in your sleep too. None of that is the problem. I know
that."

"What is?"

"Is that what you really want?" he said. "To keep writing this
column indefinitely?"

"I don't know," I said, truthfully.

"Well, I know *that* too," he said. Then he paused. "Everything has a season, my love."

I nodded. "But what does that mean I do now?"

I must have seemed like I was waiting on Peter for the answer. Only, I think we both knew, the question was more for myself than for him.

Then I thought of something. The moment that Nick told me I was priceless. It came rushing back to me. The actual moment. I had helped him rework that final scene in his movie and after he'd said, *You're priceless,* he'd said something else, something about how visual I was. And I'd thought of the green canvas box under the bed, which housed the photographs I'd taken—the hundreds and hundreds of photographs I'd taken—during all the years I'd been writing "Checking Out."

I had shown Nick some of the photographs on occasion, and he'd been mildly complimentary. Sometimes more than mildly. But in that moment, when Nick gave me that compliment, I felt brave enough to ask him what I hadn't been brave enough to ask him before: what would he think of my trying to do something with them? The photographs. Of my trying to do something with how much I loved taking them. Only, by the time I asked the question, he was already focused on his script. He was already focused on what he was trying to fix, what he was trying to do next. And so I let it go. My question. Whatever answer he would have given me.

I looked at Peter. "Maybe this will all have a happy outcome," I said. "Maybe they'll want me to do something else here? At the paper? That's always a possibility, right?"

Peter reached across the enormous impasse of the table and took my hand, squeezing it tight.

"Absolutely, but I don't think we should count on that," he

said. "It's a little like Steinbeck says, isn't it? 'We find that after years of struggle that we do not take a trip; a trip takes us.'"

As he let go, I closed my eyes.

"Peter, do you really think you still should be quoting Steinbeck?" I asked.

"No, my love," he said. "Probably not."

16

You discover this early on. Even the most upsetting, disappointing, and disheartening trips will have one great moment. Especially, in fact, on these terrible trips does the one great moment find its way to shine. The rental car breaks down in the middle of the night, the luxury hotel turns out to be a mold-infested nightmare, you get a debilitating case of the stomach flu the very moment the plane hits the ground in paradise. And yet, you go for one moonlit bike ride along the coast in Ireland, you take a hike in summertime Aspen, you wake up, healed, on the last morning in Anguilla, just in time to see the most brilliant sunrise you've ever laid your eyes on. And this rare moment of joy, especially when it is so hard-earned, feels like the entire truth. This moment of perfection makes the rest of the terrible trip worthwhile.

On the way back from New York City, the packed Amtrak train stalled twice. Once outside Stamford, Connecticut, for forty-five minutes. Then again, outside Bridgeport, for over an hour. When I finally got back to Williamsburg, it was late, almost 10:00 P.M., and the dark house made me think everyone was sleeping, or everyone but Griffin, who I assumed was still at the restaurant. I didn't blame him for this. With only a little time left until the soft opening, I'd be there as much as possible too, if I were him. To do everything I could think of to make it go as smoothly as possible.

Besides, with how overwhelmed I was feeling about every-thing—my new house, my new life, and now my new lack of employment—I almost convinced myself I was grateful for the silence.

But then I turned on the living room light to find Griffin standing there, cupping one daffodil in his right palm—the entire room behind him filled with matching daffodils in jelly jars, candles lining the bay window.

I felt a smile start to form. "What is going on in here?" I said.

He handed me my flower. "What do you mean? This is just how I plan to greet you from now on . . ." he said, a smile form-ing on his face. "A room full of flowers. Perhaps even a candle-light dinner of eggs and lobster."

I looked up at him, still a little confused. "But where is Jesse?" I asked. "And the twins?"

"I sent them away to an all-you-can feast at Pizza Hut and a triple feature in Hadley," he said. "They won't be back until later. We have the place to ourselves. We have the place to ourselves for as long as we want it. . . ."

I threw my arms around him, holding there, against his chest, as he cradled my head. His strength, coming in, filling me up.

"I'm sorry I've been at the restaurant so much. I'm sorry I haven't been around as much as I want to be."

"You don't have to be sorry. I don't want you to be sorry . . ." I said. "I got canned."

"I had a feeling."

I sighed, sitting down on the soft couch, running my fingers slowly through my hair.

Griffin sat down beside me.

"I know that there is an argument to be made that it's for the best," I said. "I mean, recently I've even thought maybe I'd be better off if I didn't have the column. And I thought that it would force the issue. Force me to figure out what I really wanted. But now that it was taken from me . . ."

"Now that it was taken from you, what?" he asked.

"Now it's what I really wanted," I said.

Griffin laughed softly, reaching over, and rubbing my back gently.

"It's going to be okay. I swear to you . . ." he said. "And I know it's probably not making it easier imagining starting again from here. I know the tip of the Berkshires is not exactly the bastion of journalistic activity."

I looked up at him, tilting my head. "Did you just say 'bastion'?"

"Yes," he said. "I thought you'd enjoy it."

I smiled at him. "I did."

"So, that's one good thing."

I laughed in spite of myself. Then I shook my head. "I just sat there, so still, the whole train ride back here, trying to figure out, what happens now? And I couldn't seem to come up with anything, like an answer."

"Well, what do you want to happen now?" he asked.

"I have no idea," I said, which was when I remembered what I'd thought about in Peter's office. That conversation with Nick. The conversation before the last conversation with Nick. The almost conversation.

"What?" he said. "I see you thinking something. What are you thinking over there?"

I shook my head. "It's silly," I said. "It's really . . . I don't know. Too silly to even mention."

"Try me."

"I've taken a lot of photographs. Since I started writing

'Checking Out.' With all the traveling, the thing that started interesting me the most was how people made a life in all these places. So I started taking photographs of . . . homes." I shrugged. "Different homes. In all the different cities I'd go to. Homes that struck me somehow. Maybe that would teach me something about how to do it, make one for myself. If that makes sense . . ."

He was quiet, for just a minute. "Do you have them here?" he said.

"The homes?"

He gave me a smile, ignoring my snarky joke. "Sure. Or," he said, "your *photographs.*"

I nodded. "They're in a canvas box. Up in the bedroom."

"Can I see them?"

"Now?"

He stood up, and reached out his hand for me to take, reached out to help me up.

"Now works for me," he said.

....

We spread them all out on the floor—all of the photographs I had taken, all the negatives, all the rolls of films that still needed developing. Six years of a secret love, staring back at us: houses in cities as distinct from each other as Hai Phong, Vietnam, and Marietta, Georgia; houses near steep cliffs in the fishing village of Klima, on the Greek island Milos, and, midrenovation, on a tiny river in Winchester, Tennessee; a lone rocking chair in front of a one-bedroom house in Cuba. We spread them all out and sat on the floor, looking at what was or wasn't there.

It took Griffin a very long time of looking at each photograph—and looking again—before he said anything.

Finally, when he did, he didn't smile. Not at first. Then he did.

"I think these are good," he said. "I think they're very good."

I gave him a disbelieving look. "That's not biased or anything."

He shook his head, his eyes back on the photographs. "Well, you can take my opinion for what it is, but I think they're strong photographs. They're interesting. And surprising. And unique." He looked right at me. "They'd make me want to know you if I didn't. Which, for me, is usually my first indication I'm around something pretty great."

I couldn't help but smile. "Is that true?" I said.

"Very, very true."

I covered my eyes in embarrassment. "Can we please change the subject now?" Then I peeked at him. "And thank you," I said.

He smiled, right at me. "You're welcome," he said.

Griffin moved the photographs gently out of the way and, less gently, pulled me toward him until my legs were around his waist, his palms cupping the back of my neck.

"I still need a plan. In my entire life, I've never *not* had a plan."

"Maybe you don't now."

"What does that mean?"

He shrugged. "I think sometimes we plan the most when we're the least sure and we want to feel okay about that. . . ." He paused. "You have something you want to do. Something you like to do. Something you're good at. Why don't we start with that? Why don't you let that be the entire plan for now?"

"I can't just . . . decide that."

He leaned forward, our faces less than an inch apart. "What if you just did?" he said.

I kissed him. I kissed him softly and sweetly. Then I did it again.

"I really love you," I said.

"I really love you back," he said.

He started to undress me, slowly at first, and then more frantically. Messily. Hands cupping my neck, hands cupping my thighs. Right there on the floor by the bed. The bed too far away.

And it occurred to me, all at once. It occurred to me—despite my day, despite my past days—how happy I felt. It occurred to me in that way that you already know you'll remember it later. You've already, accidently, locked it in.

And I couldn't help but think—the last of my clothing falling away, falling behind me—that that moment, between us, was turning into many things: a turning point, a new beginning to our new beginning.

What it wasn't turning into was the ideal moment to meet my mother-in-law.

17

"Hello, Griffin."

We jumped up in quick succession, Griffin's mother standing in front of us, fixed in her place, as we tried to get it together: Griffin turning and putting on his pants, me trying to pull my black dress back over my chest. Unable to find the strap, awkwardly holding the dress there. Hearing the zipper close on Griffin's jeans. Trying not to die at that sound.

Griffin's mother, on the other hand, didn't look embarrassed at all. She was standing there in our bedroom doorway, looking surprisingly elegant, for midnight, in a pencil skirt, looking like the original incarnation of her children—Griffin's skin, Jesse's beautiful eyes. Her own silver hair falling just above her small shoulders.

"Mrs. Putney," I said. "Or should I call you Emily?"

She looked at me head-on, and didn't answer. It didn't matter. I was apparently going to keep talking, talking in the way I did when I was compensating, desperately trying to change a moment from what it was turning out to be.

"It's so great to finally meet you," I said. "Griffin speaks of you so fondly. I can't tell you how glad I am that we are finally face-to-face."

Emily looked at me like I was speaking Russian, which I was starting to wish I was.

"Funny enough, I have a dog named Mila, which sounds a little like Emily."

Was that really how I thought I was going to turn things around? By telling her that her name sounded like my dog's?

"Is that right?" she said.

I nodded, reluctantly. "I'm not saying they rhyme or anything, though almost, I guess . . . if you say it fast enough . . . or slow enough . . ." I started to fade out. "I love her a lot."

Emily turned from me and looked at her son.

"I ran over a soccer ball in the driveway," she said. "You need lights on out there, Griff. Downlights, up in the trees. Don't you know that? It could have been a person."

"Mom, what are you doing here?" He pulled his shirt down over the part of his stomach that was still showing. "At midnight?"

I reached down for my bra, tried to push it under the bed. First with my hands, then, as I felt Emily glancing back in my direction, far more awkwardly, with the side of my foot.

"I got a phone call that my sons' lives are falling apart and, so, I thought I should probably find out in person what's going on," she said. "I got in the car after tonight's lecture and here I am. As soon as possible. To find out. So start talking."

"It's complicated."

"Make it less so, if you don't mind," Emily said, her arms crossed in front of her chest.

This standoff was so strange—and I was still in so much shock at meeting his mother, who apparently thought it was appropriate to open Griffin's bedroom door unannounced, and then make demands—that it took me a minute to realize what she had said. What had gotten her there. In front of us. That her sons' lives (plural) were falling apart. Both Jesse's *and* Griffin's.

What was falling apart in Griffin's life, in her mind? He was a successful chef, opening his own restaurant for the first time. He was doing great. All that had changed was that he had married me. Which was when I started to understand that *that* was exactly her problem.

"Wait. Jesse called you?" Griffin said, surprised.

"No," she said. "And that's very comforting, let me tell you. Gia and Cheryl did. They called together."

This was when Emily Putney turned back to me. This was when she decided she wanted to deal with me.

"You must be Annie?" she said.

And then she gave me a look. She gave me a look—how can I explain it?—that made me want to say no. That made me seriously consider it. But before I could, I heard someone barreling up the stairs, covering at least two stairs at a time.

We all turned to see Jesse—out of breath, a twin under each of his arms, their faces and hands covered in tomato sauce and orange juice and powdered sugar.

"Hey Ma!" Jesse gave his mother a big smile. "I thought that was your car I saw out front! You realize that's the twins' soccer ball you crushed underneath your back tire, right?"

"Darling," she said, "of all the many questions that need answering right now, I'm not sure that is going to come first."

....

Everyone dispersed in quick succession: Emily going to put down the boys, the bigger boys heading downstairs to have a talk with her. I, meanwhile, took a shower and got into bed, not even stopping to put the photographs away, just trying to will myself to fall asleep, to make the day over.

But I couldn't. I just lay there in the dark, my eyes slowly adjusting to the sliver of moonlight coming into the bedroom, until I was making it out again. Those beautiful designs on the bedroom ceiling, the letters and numbers making up some sort of formula that I didn't yet know how to understand. This was what I was trying to do—understand that formula—when Griffin came upstairs and got into bed with me.

I expected him to say that he was sorry—sorry for his mother, sorry for the awkward intrusion into our home happening at the end of such an already tough day for me—but he was quiet, his arm over his eyes, waiting to see whether I wanted to talk. Waiting to see if I was going to say out loud what I was starting to feel inside: this was all becoming a little too much for me.

"My mother knew we were married," Griffin said, finally. "I called her when we left Las Vegas. You should know that. I called her long before that, four days after we met, and told her I wanted to marry you. Whenever you'd have me. You should know that too."

I turned toward him. "You did?"

He nodded.

"That's very sweet."

He paused. "She just knew Gia for a long time, Annie, that's the thing. They were close. Gia was always kind to her. Patient with how Emily can be," he said. "It may just take her a minute. To adjust."

"Emily or Gia?"

"Ha-ha."

"She thinks you made a big mistake, doesn't she?" I said. "I mean with me, she's worried it was the wrong move?"

"I think she's just a little confused. Confused more than worried. Because, you know, it did happen so quickly with you, after . . ."

"You were with Gia for so long?"

"Yes."

I paused then, because I might not have liked it—didn't like being on the receiving end of it—but I did get it. Emily's question. That was a question that I had, one I was a little afraid to get the answer to, if I were being honest. How could I blame Emily for wondering too?

Which was when I asked. Kind of.

"Why does she think you were able to? Commit to me? And not her? What's her theory?"

"Look, you can't take any of it personally," he continued, as though that was an answer. "My mother . . . she can have very rigid ideas of how things are supposed to be."

"Really? I didn't notice."

Griffin laughed. I couldn't help but think of when Griffin had met my mother. How kind he was about her, how generous, how he didn't want to blame her for anything. Part of me wanted to match that generosity—in terms of Griffin's mother, in terms of what her unexpected entrance was raising for me.

But I couldn't. In that moment, a bigger part of me had no desire to be generous at all. Nick's mother had loved me, had treated me like a second daughter, even *before* Nick and I had been together. Where was I starting from this time around? Apparently hoping my mother-in-law could figure out how to *stand* me.

Still, instead of going to a place where I asked Griffin to parse his mother for me further—or asking for that, and then making unfair comparisons (at least out loud) to the mothers of my past, the ones who seemed predisposed to love me from the get-go—I did the best I could do. I looked at the designs on the ceiling, the calming designs, taking them back in.

"Am I crazy," I said, "or is there some sort of blueprint to it? Like an ordering system?" By way of explanation, I pointed up above me, swirling my finger along the outlines of the designs. "The artwork on the ceiling."

Griffin froze. Only for a second. But in that second, I could see what he knew and feared was coming. More of the truth.

More of how interconnected it all still was. Something like his past, something like our present.

"They're recipes, actually."

"Recipes?" I said.

He nodded. "Recipes from the first meal I cooked professionally. When I working for a catering service near Boston."

"What are they recipes of?"

"Pork confit and peppers, a braised lamb stew. Lemon cake."

"Lemon cake sounds good right now."

I looked at the ceiling in a different light, making out the words as ingredients, the numbers as quantities, the designs between them literally like a mixing pot moving them all together. Gorgeous, and incredible.

Then I saw it, the other thing I missed—how had I missed it?—the lilt of the *l*'s reminding me of something. Reminding me of the lilt of other *l*'s I'd just recently seen. Reminding me, all at once, of where.

"Gia drew it?"

"Yes," he said. "Gia drew it."

"Did your mother help out?" I was joking. Or I was trying to joke when I said that. But then Griffin didn't answer.

I turned over and went to sleep.

18

There was an e-mail waiting for me in the morning forwarded to me from Jesse, which had been forwarded to Jesse from Cheryl, reminding all of us that I was supposed to go on the twins' field trip to Hartford that day. Claire had sent it to Cheryl, and had asked Cheryl to send along to her sister—me, apparently—followed by a smiley face. *My sister?* Cheryl wrote in her e-mail to Jesse, followed by a series of expletives far less friendly than a smiley face.

It was the last thing I wanted to do. To be at the elementary school no later than 9:15 A.M., ready to help monitor the field trip bus. No, strike that: the last thing I wanted to do was get up and begin to focus on the photographs still strewn all over the bedroom floor. No, strike that: the last thing I wanted to do was get up and deal with my husband—to go and help him at the restaurant, like I had promised—and then have to answer to the photographs on the floor. No, strike that: the last thing I wanted to do was run into my mother-in-law on the way to helping Griffin at the restaurant on the way to dealing with the photographs.

And so I let Jesse give us all a ride to school on his way to MIT to try and work on his dissertation (and avoid his mother).

But when we pulled up to the school—the minibus already in front, the twins jumping out—Gia was standing there, getting ready to board, wearing a pair of bug-shaped sunglasses. Sunglasses that would have undoubtedly looked great with her orange scarf.

"Oh man," Jesse said, just as Gia looked up and saw both of us through the car's windshield.

"What do we do?" I said.

"Wave?" Jesse said.

I, meanwhile, was stuck on the slightly less immediate problem.

"She's going? It's the Children's Museum," I said. "A children's *science* museum. Aren't there art classes she needs to teach or something?"

"Apparently not right now."

I sighed, loudly, wrapping my terrible coat more tightly around me as I opened the passenger-side car door. "Well, come on, I guess," I said.

"Come on where?"

She was still looking right at us. She was still looking right through the windshield in her bug-shaped shades.

"To say hello."

"No way." He shook his head. "Too awkward."

"Too awkward?"

"Yep."

I glared at him. "Jesse, you're seriously going to send me out there all alone?" I said.

"I'm not sending you anywhere," he said, turning the ignition back on. "If you want to make a run for it, I'm game to take you. I'll take you anywhere you want to go. Well, anywhere between here and MIT."

"Gee, how generous," I said.

"Don't mention it," he said. "I'm that kind of guy."

. . . .

It wasn't easy, but Gia and I managed to avoid each other the entire way to Hartford—me sitting all the way up front in the minibus, Gia sitting in the back, leading the kids around her in some sort of magical-singing-puzzle contest.

We managed to avoid each other at the actual museum, all morning—it was all I could do to keep my eyes on the twins and my other assigned peanuts as they raced from one accident-waiting-to-happen exhibit to the next. We even managed to avoid talking to each other as we handed out paper-bag peanut-butter lunches together in the museum lunchroom—Gia somehow managing to do it with a flourish, each kid's bag decorated with a lacy flower.

But then, right before we were set to leave the museum, to get back on the bus and make our way home to Williamsburg, we happened to take several little girls to the bathroom in the same three-minute interval. And so, at the very end of the field trip—so close to free from each other—we found ourselves face-to-face. Or, rather, side to side. In front of the sink bank, looking into the same slightly discolored mirror.

"Hey . . ." she said.

"Hey," I said. "Long day."

She nodded.

I started washing my hands quickly, trying to hurry my girls along. Then something came over me, and I decided to take a different tactic. To be something like brave.

"Look," I said, "Gia."

She met my eyes in the mirror.

"I just wanted to say how sorry I am. I'm not sure if it matters, or makes anything better, but I wanted you to know. That I didn't know about you. Or your and Griffin's . . . history. Not really, at least."

"Why would that make it any better? Griffin knew."

It wasn't a bad point.

I shrugged. "Then I'm sorry anyway," I said. "For the rest of it. For springing it on you the way I did."

She looked at me for a last second, in the mirror's reflection, before giving me a sad smile.

"That's nice of you to say," she said. "But you don't need to apologize, really. I shouldn't have walked away from you like that. It was a little melodramatic, which is not like me. I was just shocked, as you can imagine."

"Of course. Or, I should say, I can imagine now." I paused. "I didn't mean to be the one to tell you that Griffin was married."

"It's not surprising that you were," she said. "Griffin has a hard time with blame."

Then she gave me a knowing look. And, all of a sudden, I felt like I was on the opposite team than Griffin. On a team with Gia. And I didn't want to be there. I didn't want her to think I wanted to be there.

"I don't think Griffin meant to be unfair," I said. "To anyone. It doesn't feel like he had bad intentions."

"I'm sure that's true. He doesn't have a bad bone in his body. Though I'm starting to think that was part of the problem. For us, I mean."

I looked at her, in the mirror, confused.

"It was a good thing he did, leaving town for a while. Going out to California, giving me some breathing room. I have a new boyfriend now. And I'm doing well. *We're* doing well. I'm moving on with my life. I'm moving on in a way I probably should have done a long time ago. In a way I probably wouldn't have been able to do if he had stayed."

"Oh, good." I breathed in. "That is really good to hear."

"I'm not finished."

"Okay."

"I shouldn't have called Emily. That was wrong of me. But you should know something else. About Griffin. He is a good man, a very good one. But he only knows how to love broken people. He can't show up for people who are whole. That's why I lost him. I didn't need fixing anymore. Which meant we weren't just spinning our wheels, trying to keep moving in place. You know what I mean? We were actually going to have to be in it together." She turned off the faucet. "You understand what I'm saying?"

"No," I said, and shook my head because I didn't want to. I didn't want to understand, even if I did.

There was a world in which what Gia told me could be construed as the ex-girlfriend trying to poison the well. But in the world I lived in, all I knew was that she didn't seem like she was trying to be mean. Or she was trying to be a little mean, maybe, by giving me a warning that one of these days Griffin would give up on me. But she also seemed like she was trying to be honest— didn't her story, in a way, match up to Griffin's? Just from the other side? Which actually felt much worse.

"I don't know what was going on with you when you two met, but my guess is you were at a low point, no?"

She eyeballed my coat. She eyeballed my ridiculous heart-covered coat when she asked this. And from the pitying pursing of her lips, she apparently decided she had enough information to answer her own question.

"I'm not sure it's that simple," I said.

She smiled and reached for a paper towel, started to dry her hands.

"It never is," she said. "Except when it is. That's the hard part. Knowing exactly when something is as simple as can be. I'm terrible at that myself."

I nodded and started to dry off my own hands. "Right . . ."

"Also, when you have a chance, I'd like my scarf back."

Then she threw her paper towel in the trash, and exited. Leaving me to look in the mirror. All by myself.

Emily Putney was waiting there, in the parking lot, when we got back to the school. Standing outside even though it had started snowing again, standing in her perfect parka and fur-filled boots, waiting to walk the twins home and spend the afternoon with them.

From my seat in the back row, from my seat by the emergency exit, I watched as Gia jumped off the bus, and rushed over to give Emily a hug hello—her chin cupping Emily's shoulder.

As Gia pulled back, they started talking to each other, hurriedly and happily, their faces still so close together I thought they might kiss.

I tried to make out what they were saying to each other, but I couldn't. And truthfully, it didn't matter. Whatever it was, I knew it didn't began—or end—with either of them singing my praises.

"Fantastic," I said, looking at them out the window, then looking up at the emergency exit and seriously considering pulling its firm red handle, willing it to carry me out of there.

And then, as proud as I am to admit this, while they were

still busy talking, I slid off the bus—and I do mean slid: utilizing two three-foot-five-inch-tall girls as coverage, utilizing their matching Little Mermaid lunch boxes to cover my face, a Dora the Explorer backpack to block my side.

I knew I should have said hello. I should have tried to engage Emily, but I didn't have it in me. Not right then. I was too overwhelmed. And too scared about what she might or might not say, too scared it would be something else that would make Griffin feel even more like a stranger.

Instead, I took the long way home—the back roads of the back roads—not feeling the cold wind, not feeling too much of anything. Which felt like a marker of many things. A good sign, sadly, wasn't one of them.

And so I was a little out of it, and more than a little surprised to get back to the house and find someone sitting there. On the front steps. In a long, ridiculously white ski jacket—and a matching white hat, big pom-pom on top.

I walked closer to the steps, preparing to find another Putney waiting to surprise me—a Putney eager to offer another version of how I was an enormous invasion into a life that long proceeded me.

But I didn't find another Putney there in the silly, all-white ensemble, puffing out from all angles.

I found Jordan there. My Jordan. Looking more than a little like a life-size snowball.

I stood in front of her.

"I'm going incognito," she said. "I'm afraid to be spotted by anyone I don't want to be spotted by."

This, she said, instead of hello. Instead of "How are you?" This, as though it actually made any sort of sense.

"Is it really you?" I asked.

"It's really me, and it's really fucking freezing out here," she said. "I've never been this cold in my life. On top of which, I'm thinking that you and I have had a slight misunderstanding."

"What's that?"

"I said, Go *on a date* with him. Not *marry* him."

"Oh, is that what happened? I've been wondering."

She was quiet for a minute, as we looked at each other. "I also thought you said you were in Williamstown," she said. "Didn't you? I've been driving through Massachusetts all day."

"Everyone hears Williamstown," I said.

Jordan looked around herself, taking in the cold, which felt colder in the unrelenting quiet.

"I can understand why," she said.

It didn't matter that I knew I was about to get badly yelled at for disappearing on her, for flat-out ignoring her phone calls, sending shoddy e-mails in response to hers, for acting as if that was something we'd ever historically done to each other.

None of that mattered. I sat down on the step beside her, resting my head against hers. She didn't say anything, and I knew she was going to let me. She was going to let me rest there until I was ready to tell her where I'd been.

But just then, Sammy and Dexter came bounding down the road—both of them with enormous double-scoop chocolate ice-cream cones cupped in their mitten-covered hands—the matching treats dangerously close to toppling over. Emily was a good half block behind them.

Jordan looked at the boys. Then back at me. Then back at them again.

"Please," she said, "tell me they're not yours."

20

went upstairs to freshen up: put on some warm gloves, leave my wedding ring on the beside table, my fingers too thinned and red from the cold for me to wear it. Especially where we were going.

We took Jordan's rental car, and I drove us high up into the Berkshires—pointing out Griffin's restaurant (without stopping) on the way out of town, pointing out the Montague Bookmill, a charming bookstore in Deerfield (as though I'd been inside, even once), and heading to a beautiful mountain trail in Ashley Falls that I'd driven by on my only "Checking Out" trip to the area, the year before—and that I now felt compelled to pretend I visited with some frequency.

It felt important to me to show Jordan something beautiful in my new world, even if it involved subjecting both of us to two-degree weather.

From the bottom of the mountain hike, we stared up at the entire two-mile trail, into the clouds, covered in fairly recent snow, the wind moving around us increasingly quickly.

"Are you kidding me?" Jordan said.

"It's worth it," I said.

This, as though I knew.

By the time we came to the top of the mountain, we were breathless and freezing—but not too freezing to notice that it was, *in fact,* the perfect spot that I'd hoped it would be: placing us at eye level with the crystal blue sky, leaving us to look down over the trees and the untouched snow, and the frozen river far below us.

"Okay, it's stunning up here," she said. "I admit it. It's the nicest view I've ever seen."

"I know." I looked down the mountain at the beauty all around us. "It's inimitable."

We sat down on the bench and I handed her my thermos of water. "If I say I agree with you *and* that I forgive you for using the word *inimitable,*" she asked, "can we go back down the mountain now?"

I smiled. "Maybe."

She took a long sip of the water. Then she took another. "I know you think I'm going to judge you," she said.

"Not true," I said. "I think you're *already* judging me."

"So then why aren't we at a bar yet?"

I laughed, a little louder than could be mistaken for genuine. Then, she turned toward me.

"Look, Annie . . ."

"Don't start that way," I said. "Please don't start that way. In the history of the world, no one has ever said anything good to me after starting with *look, Annie.* And something tells me this isn't going to be the first time."

"I was just going to say that I get it," she said. "I do. You got screwed, royally, and made a major decision because of it. An impulsive decision. One you wouldn't have made under normal circumstances. Ever."

I tilted my head, toward her. "And how is this supposed to make me feel better?" I asked.

"I'm just saying that you're human. You wanted to be the one to move on quicker than Nick did, to prove that you're more okay. So update your Facebook page. New status: *Married*. Let them put up that dumb red heart beside it, proving to the entire world you're fine. You're happy. You're content." She paused. "Then come home."

I shook my head. "That isn't what this is about," I said. "I don't even have a Facebook page."

She gave me a look. "Then I really don't know where to start."

"Jordan, I know what this all must look like to you," I said, motioning around myself. "But I'm doing great. I'm happy. Yes, it takes a minute to fit into a new life. But that's par for the course. You can't tell me it was *all* smooth sailing when you and Simon got married. Not with Sasha and his ex-wife and all the rest of it."

"It was smoother than this."

I shook my head. "I'm happy," I said.

"So you keep saying."

"Then what's the problem?"

She looked right at me. "If you're so happy," she said, "then why do you look so sad?"

That stopped me. And, before I knew it, I was crying. I was sitting with my oldest friend on top of a crazy mountain, crying about all of it. Losing my job and being inundated by Griffin's crazy family and being hated by his *Town & Country* ex-girlfriend and living in a town that felt like everyone else's home but mine. I cried about how, in all the craziness, I felt disconnected from him. And from myself.

"The truth is that I get that the restaurant is opening soon," I said. "I knew that was going to be the deal. But on top of everything that's going on, it's just making me feel . . ."

"Like you don't belong here?" she asked.

I shrugged. "A little like I may not belong anywhere."

Jordan looked confused, but I wasn't sure how to say it out loud so that it made more sense than that. I was just becoming keenly aware in all the movement in my life recently—all the movement forever, really—I'd never stopped long enough to know what was going to make me happy. To know the difference between moving around and getting somewhere. And now that I had come to a full stop, what if I didn't have the tools to hold on to it—something like stability, like happiness—even if I wanted to?

"So," Jordan said. "Here's the other thing maybe you can help me wrap my head around. How does the girl who goes to Williams-Sonoma *seven* times before purchasing a coffeepot end up married to someone whose middle name she doesn't even know?"

"Griffin doesn't have a middle name."

"That you know," she said.

That made me laugh, for real this time. I started wiping at my tears, trying to pull it back together.

"You've got no one to blame but yourself," I said. "You're the one who told me to be the opposite of myself."

"I don't remember saying that."

I looked at her, dazed. The basis of the whole new me, the advice that I was certain was going to save my life, and she didn't even remember giving it.

"That is going to kind of hurt your credibility for a while," I said.

"Let me just ask you one more question then," she said. "Do you love him?"

I didn't have to pause, not even for a second.

"Yes," I said. "Very much."

At the end of everything I told her, there was also that. Maybe I had fallen into this life on some kind of impulse, resulting from my last one falling so stupendously apart, resulting from my feeling like I had something to prove in the aftermath of that. But there was this too. I loved Griffin. With all of my heart. However I had gotten here, I felt that in my core. Which immediately made me feel better.

But then Jordan pulled her hat down lower on her head, shielding her eyes.

"Then if that's true, or you *think* that that's true, you're going to have to work really hard to hear this," she said. "You need to leave him."

"Excuse me? Did you hear what I just said?"

"Did *you* hear what you just said?" she asked. "This isn't the right life for you, Annie. Stuck in the middle of nowhere. *Stuck* anywhere. You need freedom. And lots of it."

"Says who?"

"Everyone!"

"Maybe *everyone* should spend more than ten minutes inside of my life before making that assessment," I said. "Maybe freedom is just another word for nothing left to lose."

She tilted her head. "Did you really just quote Janis Joplin?"

"Maybe!" I said, gathering steam. And volume.

In response, Jordan got calmer and quieter, like she was talking to a crazy person, like that crazy person was me.

"All I'm saying is this is a reversible error," she said. "You can get it annulled. I can do that for you."

I shook my head, feeling myself getting mad. "I really can't believe you," I said.

"Why are you so defensive, then?" she asked. "If I'm not at least a little right, there's no reason to be defensive."

"You're wrong," I said, standing up, anxious to get away from her before it was too late, knowing we were about to go there. To the place where we both went too far and were inevitably sorry later.

"Where are you going?" she said.

"I don't want to talk to you about this anymore," I said. "I would never talk about your life that way."

"Well, I'm not you. I'm a royal bitch, at least some of the time. But that's not news. Also not news: I love you more than anything. And don't pretend for a second you doubt that all of a sudden. This is about you, and what's good for you. This isn't about my brother."

I looked down at her. "He's your brother again?"

She had no trouble holding my gaze. "My point's the same either way, Annie. I want for you what you want for yourself."

I motioned around myself at the interminable mountain. "*This* is what I want for myself," I said. "Did it occur to you that just maybe I found exactly what I've always wanted?"

"Since when is this what you wanted?" she said. "I'm sorry, but I won't sit around and let you get away with getting less than what you really want: *till death do you part.* Just because during a moment of Nick's slight confusion, you decided it was the right decision to move to the middle of nowhere with Chef Boyardee."

I didn't know where to start, with all of that, but I shored myself up to start somewhere. "First of all, this is not the middle of *nowhere*," I said. "There is a state university nearby, if you didn't notice."

"There is also a *farm* museum nearby, if *you* didn't notice."

I turned and started walking away from Jordan, started walking through the thick snow toward the entrance to the trail that would lead me back down the mountain and away from her.

I could feel Jordan behind me, struggling to keep up, and then stopping in her tracks. Coming to a full stop.

"It's over with Pearl, by the way," she called out, after me. "In case you're interested. It was over before it even started."

I didn't turn around. I didn't keep going, holding in place exactly where I was, but I didn't turn around either.

Then I could hear Jordan's footsteps start again, as she moved closer, until she was standing right behind me.

"He's in London, finishing up his project. And trying to line up whatever work he can get all over Europe, and trying not to be as miserable as he is. It's pathetic, really. But he says he can't go home without you. He *won't.*"

I still just stood there, Jordan lowering her voice.

"Look," she said. "He knows how royally he screwed up. But he told me that he's not going to just show up and tell you so, not if I tell him you're happy. But if I tell him you're not . . ."

I turned around fast to look at her, fury filling my eyes. "Don't do that, Jordan," I said. "I'm not kidding. That's the last thing I need right now."

"Then tell me it doesn't matter to you," she said. "That *six months ago* he was the love of your life, but now it doesn't matter to you."

"It was more than six months ago."

"I'm sorry, my mistake. *Seven* months ago."

I turned away from her and started walking again. "It doesn't matter to me," I said.

"You want to say that while looking at me?" she said. "I'm thinking it'd be more effective."

I kept going, right down the cold mountain.

"I don't like you very much right now," I said.

"Well, it's a good thing," she called after me, "I can live with that."

21

Jordan didn't stay over. She drove back to New York City and was planning to take the first flight out to Los Angeles the next morning. She said she was going to stay by the airport, but I wondered if *airport* was friend code for spending a day or two in New York City or Boston or anywhere but with me in rural Williamsburg, before heading home to California. Whether or not that was true, she might as well have stayed with me. Right in the house. In my bedroom. Her words kept echoing in my head as loudly if she were right beside me. As if she were still saying them in real time. *You shouldn't stay here.*

This was at least part of the reason why, after she'd gone, I went over to the restaurant to help Griffin. I thought going there was the wise thing to do—to be with him, try to feel reconnected, and get focused on helping him with the endless preparations for opening night. But with Jordan's words in my head, I'm not sure why I didn't understand that the wise thing, right then, would have been to stay away.

We started setting up the outside lights—the beautiful,

lotus-shaped lights, white and sparkly—stringing them up on the roof and the front brick, vinelike.

"I can't believe the opening is a week away," I said.

"Ten days!" he said.

"Ten days," I corrected myself.

I was standing on a stepladder, Griffin beneath me, holding out a lantern to aid us in seeing a little better. He had been asking me about Jordan. He had been asking me in ways that were making it hard to avoid telling him what had happened, unless I blatantly managed to change the topic.

"And it's only the soft opening," he said.

"I don't care. It's still exciting. And didn't you tell me the test run is almost more important than anything else? That it sets the tone?"

"Are you trying to freak me out, or is that just happening naturally?" he said.

I laughed. "Well, maybe it would relax you a little if we actually picked a name for the restaurant. Have you been thinking?"

"I've been thinking . . ." he said. "I'm getting closer. But, in case we don't hit on it in the next week, the good news is that everyone who is coming to the soft opening knows where to go."

"We do have that on our side, I guess."

He smiled up at me in the lantern light. "Still, if I'd known Jordan was here, I would have taken a break for a little while . . ." he said. "I'm sorry that I didn't get to spend any time with her."

I turned from him, turned from that smile, focused on my lights.

"Maybe it's not the end of the world," I said.

"Well, I'd hope not," he joked. "But she matters to you. And I want to know her."

I felt my chest clench in that moment, at that kindness. It was a small kindness, but it was so genuine. So much like Griffin.

And, if anything, it should have moved me closer to him, closer to what I knew to be true about him, not closer to Jordan's words.

But it didn't. Because, rationally or not, all I was thinking was, *why, despite that, does our life not feel complete enough to show her?*

"Don't forget that she's Nick's sister," I said.

"So?"

"Her allegiance is to him."

Griffin drilled me with a look that I could make out, even in the dim lantern light.

"What?" I said.

"I don't know," he said. "I thought we were playing way past that kind of allegiance."

That was the moment that I should have said, *of course we are.* But I was already heading somewhere far less productive. "Maybe you should ask Gia about that," I said. "Or your mother."

"Annie . . ."

I lowered the lights. "You don't get it," I said.

"No, clearly not," he said. "But the good news is that I'm not dumb. I mean I'm not always the smartest guy in the room, but I've been known to get *it*. *It* and I have a really good relationship, most of the time."

He was trying to make light of things. I wasn't having it though. I didn't want it to be light. I wanted it to be heavy. Suddenly, I wanted it to be so heavy that *it* would have no choice but to break.

My hands started to shake, the lights moving like cylinders inside of them, as I stepped off the ladder. Griffin was getting dangerously close to doing it. To reaching for me, which I couldn't let him do. Because it would be the last straw, feeling his hands on me. And it might stop me from doing it, what I felt myself already doing. Finding reasons to burn the house down.

He must have sensed my hesitation in moving color because he pulled back, reached into the bucket, picked out some more lights. And started to talk.

"So I was thinking about you almost all day today. I mean,

more accurately, I was thinking about your photographs," he said. "And I had this idea. It may be a little nutty, but it may also be great . . . did you look at them again today?"

"No."

He nodded. "Well, we should probably talk about it when they're in front of us, but my idea . . ."

"You know, maybe it's a little soon for ideas, Griffin," I said. "And maybe we should both start anticipating that I'm going to get nowhere with all of this photography stuff."

"That's a good attitude," he said.

He paused, as I shrugged—shrugged as if to say, *sorry, but it's the only one I've got right now.*

"Annie, you have talent. And you can do something here. *We* can do something. We'll figure it out, together."

Figure it out together. All of a sudden, Gia's words came back to me: *Griffin only knows how to love broken people.*

"I don't need saving, Griffin," I said.

He gave me a confused look. "Who said anything about you needing saving?" he asked.

"No one," I said. And then, before I could stop myself: "Gia did, actually. Or, rather, she shared that *that* part of a relationship is a hobby of yours."

"Gia is wrong about that. Which maybe is my fault." He paused, a look of shame coming over his face. "I didn't want to disappoint her, so I stayed in the relationship too long. But I wasn't trying to save her. I loved her. I was trying to fix our relationship, which is a different thing. It made me willing to do the work for too long after I shouldn't have been, after I knew we probably weren't going to get to where we needed to be."

He met my eyes and I had to admit what he was saying sounded like the truth—or at least the truth as far as he understood it. So why, even with evidence banking up on our side of things, did I not feel any calmer?

"It was never about saving Gia, Annie," he continued. "And it certainly isn't about that with you."

"Well, then what is about then, Griffin? Because I'm just saying we can put together whatever plan you want, but I'm probably better off preparing for the fact that my photography is just a hobby," I said. "And I'm most likely going to end up jobless in this town unless I take a job writing for the *Boondocks Bee*."

My tone stopped him, pulling him away from him whatever was left of his understanding.

"What did Jordan say to you today, Annie?" he asked.

"Nothing . . ." I said.

"Then why do you want to fight with me so badly? Why is that, apparently, the only thing that's going to make you feel better?"

I was already heading away, not stopping to drop the lights back into their bucket—the small, innocent lights that I was still squeezing between my fingers, that had nothing to do with any of this.

"It's not," I said. "That's not what I'm doing."

"Then what are you doing?"

"I'm just going home," I said.

It occurred to me, as I said it, that maybe my biggest problem of all was that I still wasn't at all sure where that was.

22

Something that always shocked me, during the years that I was writing "Checking Out," was how many letters I'd regularly receive from readers asking me about how they could get out of a trip they no longer wanted to take. How they could get out of a trip that they'd known, in advance, was not refundable. I never knew what made them think I would have that answer. Then, after time, I realized that most of the readers didn't really want that answer. They didn't even really want *out*. Not of that trip they had been planning for, hoping for, and waiting for. But like whenever you feel your options close in—even if they close in on what you were aiming to find—those looking to cancel still wanted to feel like they had the option of out. That it wasn't a fait accompli, everything that was coming. That there was a back door they *could* find their way to, whether or not they were going to use it.

When I got back to the house, there was a note from Emily waiting for me on the kitchen table.

Annabelle,

I was hoping to talk with you before I left, but I need to get back to Manhattan for an early class tomorrow morning. Soon?

—Emily

I put the note back down wondering what she was hoping to talk to me about. All the other things I didn't understand about her son? About what he needed? All the other things we should have thought about before falling into a life together?

The leftovers of the dinner she had served the twins were also on the table: barbeque chicken fingers and sweet-potato curly fries, blueberry-banana milk shakes.

I picked up a handful of fries and headed slowly up the stairs, dragging myself toward our bedroom, feeling completely hammered from my arguments. The one with Jordan that I didn't ask for. The one with Griffin that I insisted upon.

I was relieved when I passed the twins' room to see that the door was shut, the lights off. And I was even more relieved when I passed the bathroom, the shower water clearly running, an occupied Jesse's loud hums audible from the hallway.

I had ample evidence, all of a sudden, that I would be getting through the rest of my waking hours alone and unscathed.

Then I headed into my own bedroom and saw it: I'd been wrong. Wrong about the evidence. And wrong about the leftovers of dinner. They weren't just on the kitchen table. They were all over the bedroom floor. In shades of barbeque red. Sweet-potato orange. In bright blueberry milk shake.

They were all over the floor, and all over my photographs. All of my photographs.

Ruined.

"Now, that's not good."

I don't know how long I was standing there, frozen, when I turned to find Jesse in the doorway, in jeans and a T-Shirt—ATOM spray-painted across the shirt's front—his hair still wet from his shower.

"No," I said.

"And probably not the best moment," he said, "but I feel like I should also tell you that Sammy *may* have swallowed your wedding ring."

"May have?"

"My only source is Sammy," Jesse said. "Who also told me he swallowed the kitchen table."

I turned back to look at my bedside table, and saw what was notably missing: my thin, gold ring. I moved closer to the table, looking for the gold's gleam in the carpet, underneath the table legs. It was nowhere.

And then, from my new vantage point, I took in once again the disaster that was now my maybe-not-future. The photographs. The negatives. The scrunched film rolls. The canvas box swimming in a blueberry puddle.

"You want some help cleaning this up?" Jesse asked.

I looked right at him.

"I want some help," I said, "getting anywhere else."

....

We sat on the porch steps, like it wasn't the dead of winter—me on the bottom one, Jesse on the top, a bottle of bourbon on the step between us—and proceeded to get drunk, looking up at the star-filled sky, letting the liquor help fight the cold, waiting for Griffin to get home.

We got so drunk that I ended up telling Jesse all of it, about the end of my relationship with Nick, about losing my column, about the craziness that had been that very day: from Gia and her terrible bathroom confessional to Jordan and Chef Boyardee.

I told him all of it, and apparently in an amusing way, because he was hysterically laughing.

He was laughing so hard, by the end, that he made me tell him the Chef Boyardee part twice.

"I'm glad my life is so humorous to you," I said.

"Wow," he said, wiping at his eyes, fighting back a final laugh. "It really, really is."

I kept shaking my head, but I couldn't really pretend to be offended. I was laughing too.

"So is Jordan always such a bitch?" Jesse said.

"Hey! That's not entirely fair," I said.

"I think it is, actually."

"She's just worried about me," I said. "You know, she thinks I've gone off the deep end."

"What if you have?"

I reached for the bottle of bourbon and took another swig, letting it fall down my throat, burning it.

"I see three of you, so it's not entirely surprising that I'm not exactly following but . . . I'm not exactly following."

"I'm saying, what if Jordan's right that you've gone off this so-called deep end? Why does that leave you any worse off than before?"

I held the bottle out for him to take. "How's that's supposed to make anything better?"

"It just seems to me that the deep end was where you were headed. One way or the other. Even if you had stayed in that halfway house of a life in L.A." He paused. "The question is, what are you going to do about it now? Ignore what you know, or pick something that counts?"

I was having a little too much trouble following that too, which was when—in my lucidless haze—I started to wonder who he was really talking to with his little speech: me or him.

"Are you worried she's not going to forgive you?" I said. "Once the dust has settled, and everyone's calmed down? Are you worried Cheryl isn't going to be able to try again?"

Jesse took another long drink, swallowing slowly. "Cheryl's not the one I'm worried about."

I looked at him, confused. "You're worried about Jude Flemming?" I said.

"I'm worried about Jude Flemming," he said. "After all, she's really the wronged person in this scenario."

"How so?"

"We got involved when I was at a very bad moment, very bad for anybody wanting something from me," he said. "Cheryl and I had just separated and . . ."

"Wait, you separated from Cheryl before Jude?"

"Yeah."

"Jude Flemming wasn't the cause?"

He shook his head. "Not at all. She thought she was going to be my answer, though," he said. "She was *convinced* she was going to be my answer. And, then, I guess I could be hers too. Except for the fact that I never stopped wanting to be with my wife, which I tried to be incredibly clear about. She's still not hearing me on that point."

"Wait, which she?"

"Take your pick."

I didn't know what to say to that.

He took a long slug from bourbon bottle. "And the worst part is, Jude and I only had sex one time. *Relations.* One time, and she's pregnant." He paused. "We're like an after-school special. The elderly version."

This stopped me.

"But . . ." I shook my head, totally confused. "Then why were you separated from Cheryl in the first place?"

"I'd gotten her yoga lessons for her birthday. Private yoga lessons. With Theodore. Just Theodore. One name. Like Madonna. Can you believe that crap? He's supposed to be the best yoga teacher in

Boston though. And I never seemed to get her anything she liked for her birthday, so, against my better judgment, I hired him."

"Okay."

"Let's just say that, this year, I finally got my wife something she liked for her birthday."

My eyes opened wide. "Cheryl and Theodore?"

"Cheryl and Theodore. Though, if you believe her, it isn't physical between them. How do you even compete with that? After all, if she's getting so much from Theodore *emotionally*, doesn't that say something about what she wasn't getting from me?"

I couldn't help but think of Nick—Nick and his emotional match, Pearl. How *do* you compete with that? With the possibility of what *might* be? I didn't even know how to try.

"Jesse, I'm so sorry," I said.

He ran his fingers through his hair. "Now she doesn't know what she wants. She came back to me for a minute, she left again," he said. "She talked about coming back another time, then felt like she wasn't ready."

"What does ready look like in that scenario?"

He shrugged. "Cheryl and I . . . we'd been together since we were sophomores at MIT, and she was studying botany. I took three horrible plant and soil classes just to be near her. . . ." He shook his head. "I guess it's hard sometimes to last . . . when you've lasted."

I took back the bourbon bottle. I held it by my mouth, feeling floored. I wanted to reach out and touch him and tell him it was going to be okay. But I also knew I had no idea if that was true so instead, I put down the bottle, and looked back up. At the stars. At the midnight sky.

"Man," I said, "you sure know how to put someone else's problems into perspective."

He started to laugh, all over again. And then I was laughing too. "Glad to help," he said. "But I wouldn't be too high and mighty if I were you."

"Why's that?" I said.

"I know what I want. I'm just trying to figure out how to get there."

I started to ask what he knew he wanted—to go back to Cheryl? Be there to help Jude? But before I could get there, he kept talking.

"You, Annie Adams," he said, "are still a mountain's worth of walking behind all that."

I wanted to argue that that wasn't true—that I knew exactly what I wanted. I wanted to be with Griffin, and make my life work here. I wanted to stay. But in my head, my admittedly bourbon-soaked head, Griffin came out as Nick. So I knew saying the rest out loud was probably not the wisest move right then.

"But consider this," Jesse said, picking the bourbon back up, "maybe you aren't in this position because you forgot yourself, but because you started getting honest about who you really might be."

Before I could say anything to that, Jesse tilted the bourbon my way.

"Welcome to the deep end," he said.

The next morning I woke up to the telephone ringing—ringing in a desperate way that let me know it was certainly not the first time the telephone had rung, not the first time the caller was trying to get through.

My head was spinning from leftover bourbon and not enough sleep. As I reached for the phone, I slowly started to realize what was happening around me: that I was in the bedroom alone, Griffin's side of the bed not slept in, yet my mostly destroyed photographs no longer strewn across the floor, and somehow cleaned up.

Then, suddenly, all I could do was focus on lying very still, the bourbon moving around my stomach, dangerously close to coming up the wrong way. The phone mercifully stopped ringing.

And then it started again. Because I was in no position to think of another way to make the ringing stop, I picked up.

"Hello?" I said.

"Are you ready to start singing to me?"

"What?"

"I think you should sing to me that Bette Midler song, the

one about the unsung hero. The one who holds up your wings? Or if you prefer, you can sing the one by that girl who won *American Idol*. About having a moment in the sun."

It was Peter. It was Peter, former editor extraordinaire, who was on the other end of the phone making these terrible references to easy listening songs.

My arm was covering my eyes, my elbow pointing straight up, fighting the spinning in my head.

"Peter," I said. "My head is spinning so badly you are coming out as an echo. Can I call you back?"

"Absolutely not. Not when I've been calling you incessantly for the last two hours to tell you the great news." He paused for effect. "You are unfired!"

I moved my arm off my eyes. "What?"

"There has been an uproar in your absence. Well, uproar may be a bit strong, but the point is that they want you back, my love. They want you and they want me. Thanks to the minor uproar and some crafty maneuvering on my part. *The A-Team!* Peter and Annie. Back in business!"

"I can't believe it."

"You're not the only one!" he said. "But, *now*, before you get all excited, you need to know 'Checking Out' is still over. At least in its former incarnation. Caleb Number Two wants to create a real-time travel column. More interactive in a variety of ways that are still to be determined. Though regardless of the details, you'll like this part. They'll be paying you more."

"Really?"

"Don't even get me started on how I pulled that off. Just, if anyone ever asks you, a little magazine called *National Geographic* was very interested in having you head their African Bureau."

"Okay . . ."

"My love, I can go over all the details with you later, but the main thing you need to know is that I got you a three-year contract. A thirty-three percent *raise,* right off the bat, full health benefits back. And they want much more involvement from you. They want you to help the paper create a *travel presence.* Whatever that is supposed to mean, *TBD,* as they say. But, of course, considering the ongoing micromanaging reign of terror, there's the small issue that they need you to do it from London. Though they will be giving you housing while you acclimate. One of the benefits of being taken over by a massive corporate conglomerate, I suppose."

"Wait. Slow down a sec. What do you mean, London?"

"My love, if you don't know what I mean by London, I may have to reconsider fighting so hard for your job."

I got quiet. I didn't know what else to do. "I live in Massachusetts," I said.

"I know you live in Massachusetts, but Beckett Media is very serious about their European bureau. They're even considering sending me over for a spell," he said. "They wanted you based out of London, or out of Berlin. Those were the choices. And, let's be honest, I'm not sure you're cool enough to live in Berlin."

"Thanks a lot," I said.

"All I'm saying is, it's not forever," he said. "Can't you commute home for the time being?"

"From *London?*"

"Go back on the occasional weekend, perhaps. For the occasional silly Hallmark holiday."

"Peter . . ."

"It's a great opportunity," he said. "Perhaps, one could say, a once-in-a-lifetime opportunity."

"What happened to *everything has a season?*" I said. "What happened to your whole speech that my heart wasn't in 'Checking Out' anymore? That it might be time to move on?"

"I would have said anything to make you feel better!" he said. "And this is London, we're talking about. You *love* London. And, keep in the back of your head, you can always make a demand later about returning to America, once they know how much they need you. Six months, and you'll be good to head back out to Farm Town, USA. Nine at the most."

"Peter . . ."

"Farmland?"

"I can't, Peter. I just can't right now. . . ."

"You can."

I shook my head. I shook my head as though he could see me. And then I said the truth, my queasy stomach seconds away from a win.

"Right now all I can do is get off the phone."

. . . .

An hour later I was opening the door to Griffin's restaurant. I didn't know how to begin to process the job news, but I knew I had to see Griffin, to make last night right, or more right. I needed to explain to him what was happening with me. And maybe by doing so, I could start to understand.

But when I walked inside, I felt at a loss all over again. Because sitting at the newly completed bar—sitting on one of the beautifully brushed stools in front of it—was Gia. Gia leaning across the bar top, leaning across her tall mug of coffee, toward Griffin, who was leaning toward her too, both of them laughing. Both of them looking happy, together.

I stopped in my tracks. I stopped in my tracks, just as they simultaneously turned to look at me.

"Annie . . ." Griffin said.

And Gia waved.

Uncertain what to do, I waved too, a small hip-side one. Then I hurried—too fast for it to seem natural—right back out of the front door.

Griffin followed me outside, calling after me, and I thought seriously about not turning around. But I had to. For starters, I had walked the wrong way and had no idea where I was going.

"Will you slow down, please? Annie, come on . . ." Griffin said, putting his hand on my arm.

"I'm sorry," I said. "I didn't mean to interrupt."

"That was not what she looked like," he said.

That stopped me. "What it looked like," I said. "*It*. That's what you meant to say."

"What did I say?"

"You said she."

I wasn't sure how to explain why that felt worse. Maybe because even when it wasn't supposed to be about other people for us, it was starting to feel like it was becoming that.

"Annie, please just listen to me for a second. I see where you are going, but I need you to listen to me. Gia had an argument with her boyfriend," Griffin said. "She wanted to talk to me, get some guidance. That's all."

"She wanted to get some guidance from you?" I said. "About her new boyfriend?"

He nodded. "He's not behaving all that well."

He's not the only one, I wanted to add.

"Griffin, do you really think you're the best person for her to be confiding in about that?"

"I know it sounds silly," Griffin said. "But it's a good thing. It's a good thing for us to be talking to each other. A good thing for all of us. Putting the past in the past, you know that?"

I shook my head because I didn't know that. What I did know was that everything was blurring together in my mind, past lives and present ones: Gia and Nick and Griffin and me, Jesse and Cheryl and Jude. "Checking Out" and photography and "Checking Out" again. There was supposed to be a boundary parting them: the past, the present, the time I didn't understand what I needed for myself, the time I did. The time I felt like I had to keep escaping, the time I wanted to stay still.

"Will you come back inside?" Griffin said. "It's freezing out here." He had his arms wrapped around himself, proving the point.

I was still too stung. But I let him know in spite of that, and maybe a little because of it, what I had done.

"I sent an e-mail out for you this morning," I said. "I sent an e-mail out to all my former colleagues at the paper. All the food critics I know, the style editors, the arts columnists, everyone, letting them know about the restaurant's soft opening. Inviting them to come then, or anytime in the next few months. As our guests. I thought you'd want to know that."

"I do," he said. "Thank you."

Then I started walking, the right way this time.

Griffin called after me. "Where are you going?"

But I couldn't say the words. Only he seemed to understand part of what I wasn't saying, because he moved closer to me.

"You're my choice, Annie. You have been since day one." He paused. "Even if you pretend not to, I know you know that. And I know I'm your choice too."

I shook my head, refusing to let it be that simple. "You keep saying the past is the past," I said. "But it doesn't feel past to me when it is immeasurably locked into the present. Then it's something else."

"What's that?" he said, his voice tensing up. "An excuse to walk away?"

"At the very least," I said, even as I knew it wasn't helping anything, "it's a reason to end this conversation."

. . . .

That night, when Griffin came home, I pretended to be asleep. I lay there, perfectly still, while he moved around the bedroom, getting undressed and washing up, moving beneath the covers, settling in himself.

He put his arm over his eyes, not saying anything. Not to me.

And I remembered the first night we spent together—or, rather, the morning after. How I had tried to pretend I was sleeping then too. How he hadn't bought it. And how he'd gone ahead and done it: the one thing I most needed him to do. He moved toward me.

Maybe that made it my turn, this time.

Eight inches. Griffin was eight inches away. I'd traveled clear around the world twice. I'd been to Dubai three times; Hong Kong, four. I'd found the tiniest town in New Zealand, which takes three days to get to by boat, and, then, only if you know exactly where you are going.

I could get as far away as possible.

And still. I couldn't figure out how to move eight lousy inches toward the person I needed most.

24

A few days later, I did something I didn't ever think I'd do. I drove all the way out to Amherst, to the library at the state university there, to write my final column for "Checking Out." The column was focused on Las Vegas—a city that, despite its close proximity to Los Angeles, I had avoided writing about the entire duration of the time I worked on the column. I picked several things about Las Vegas, several things that would make it a trip worth embarking on—a place where you'd want to escape. They included a beautiful hike out in Red Rock Canyon (for "Open Your Eyes"), an underground Korean restaurant ("Find the Special Sauce"), a bizarrely interesting lake community ("Take the Wrong Exit), and a private downtown casino—far from the strip—that was open only after midnight, and housed Edward, the longest-running blackjack dealer in Vegas, who had been dealing blackjack hands for seventy-one years ("Leave Your Comfort Zone").

And then, for the final one ("Discover the One Thing You Can't Find Anywhere Else"), I chose something personal, the first and only personal thing I'd really shared about myself in the entirety of writing my column. I wrote about the chapel, the small chapel with orange shutters right on the Las Vegas city border, where you could have a quiet wedding, quieter then the rest of Las Vegas would certainly allow. Where the in-house chaplain would give you sweet bouquets of white and green flowers, and raspberry-infused champagne. He'd also give you a moment alone. Before and after the service.

But I didn't write down any of that. What I wrote was this: *Because it's where I married my husband.*

I hit SEND, and left the library quickly. Or, I should say, I intended to leave the library quickly. But, on the way out, I saw it—on a pole right by the main door—a poster announcing MOVIE NIGHT in the Student Commons. And the movie they were showing. *Roman Holiday.*

I can't explain exactly why I went over to the commons to watch it, why I gave in to my need to get lost in its comfort. Maybe because I felt so emptied right then, so very tired. Maybe because I felt something else, something more precarious— that tricky mix of lost and found—which, I was learning, meant I was entering the final moment where both outcomes were equally possible.

I got to the commons halfway through the movie, in time to see Joe Bradley and Princess Ann sitting together by the incredible Spanish Steps, as he convinced her to step outside herself and do the things she'd always most wanted to do—take a disallowed adventure through Rome's glorious streets and cafés; ride a motorcycle and go dancing; find the magical wall where wishes came true. To give in, if just once, to her own heart.

I got there in time to see Ann sitting in Bradley's car at the end of their adventure, looking dazzling and alive and brutally resolved, saying good-bye to her one love.

*I have to leave now. I'm going to that corner there and turn.
You must stay in the car and drive away. Promise not to
watch me go beyond the corner. Just drive away and leave
me, as I leave you.*

I got there in time for all of that. And I stayed until the very
end, enjoying every single second.

And, forty-eight hours later, Nick came to take me home.

....

Part 3

Happily Ever After . . . Take 2

You may do this, I tell you, it is permitted.
Begin again the story of your life.

—JANE HIRSHFIELD

25
....

I t was the morning of Griffin's restaurant opening and I decided it all came down to this: I needed to remember. Before I opened my eyes, I needed to remember—no, I needed to *know*—five things about this room. Five was a good number. It clearly counted as several, counted as many. I needed to prove to myself that waking up in someone's house, someone's house who was apparently my husband, waking up in a bedroom I had committed to living my life in, I knew *many* things about it for certain. From memory. From some place deep inside myself. Then, maybe, this was my home. Then I could decide what to do next.

Number one. On the wall across from the bed, there was a black-and-white photograph of the Strand Theater in Keyport, New Jersey. A beautiful photograph of the theater's side view, taking up most of the wall. It was a photograph Griffin's mother had taken, which he'd blown up and framed himself. She had taken it when Griffin was a kid, during a summer the family had spent down on the New Jersey Shore. Griffin told me he remembered standing there, beside his mother, when she took it. He remembered because it was the first time all day she hadn't insisted that he and Jesse stand in the frame too. She'd wanted the theater alone. I had seen a remarkably similar photograph of the theater in the window of an art gallery in Venice Beach. It had struck me, even then, but I hadn't gone inside to look at it closely. So maybe I was remembering wrong. What I thought had struck me, what I thought I'd seen. What I thought was connecting Griffin and me, even before we were connected.

Number two. Large glass doors covered the left wall of the bedroom, two beautiful french doors that led out to a balcony. This was my favorite part of the room. My favorite part of the house. Those doors, that balcony. The house—its sweet Craftsman quality—felt built around it. Griffin put a wicker rocking chair out there, and I loved sitting in it and looking out, toward the backyard, the forest, the river beyond it. The two times I had.

Number three. There was a desk in the corner of the room, an iron desk—slanted, like an artist's desk, but with a slender drawer. A drawer that had a gold knob, which I had assumed would open the drawer. I'd assumed wrong. When I turned the knob, it fell off. I'd hidden it in the sock drawer. That tiny gold knob. Hidden the minor crime. And I still hadn't told Griffin. I still hadn't gotten around to telling him that either.

Number four. The walls were painted a pale blue. Not an ocean blue, not a deep royal blue. Softer than all of that. Griffin had these soft blue walls that looked lovely with his brown curtains, a combination that couldn't help but draw your eyes upward, toward the sky itself. Toward Gia's incredible design, living there. Still living right above me.

I opened my eyes. I was out. At four, I was out. I had thought there were two matching nightstands—iron and tilted, like the desk—but that was wrong. When I opened my eyes, I saw that there was only one. By my side. The side that ate my wedding ring. On the other side, on Griffin's, there was a small table. His ring resting there, safe.

So there I was. At number four. Four was better than three. It wasn't five, but it was better than three. So why was my heart pounding so loudly, and so hard, that it was starting to hurt? Why was I panicking? And what did it mean that, as much as I tried to push the question aside, it kept coming back: *How could I stay here?*

Because there was this: There was a number five that I knew, only it belonged to me. My suitcase, by the bedroom door, still packed. And ready to be used. In a matter of minutes, ready to come with me out of here.

Just then, my eyes on the suitcase, Griffin reached out, and put his arm around me. His arm was surprisingly heavy—were many men's arms this heavy? Nick's certainly wasn't. I didn't remember ever having an arm around me that was that heavy— that sturdy, that ready. Ready, in its strength, to try and keep me safe. His arm had this long vein, running down the middle, not in a straight line, but a jagged one, like the line in the middle of a graph, measuring stocks, or the weather in North Dakota over a five-year period. And when I turned his arm over, I would see on his wrist half a tattoo. Half an anchor tattoo—half his history. And, now, mine.

Griffin's arm around me—the way it felt—this part, I already knew by heart.

26

G riffin decided it came down to the music. The success or failure of the restaurant's opening came down, he announced, to the perfect mix of the nine seminal albums he was compiling into one mix, music ranging from *Astral Weeks* to *Boxer* to *18 Tracks* to *In the Aeroplane over the Sea* to *The Blue Album* to *End of Amnesia* to *I'm Your Man*. Music that would seep into the way he prepared the food, that would seep into the way everyone tasted it.

We spent so long trying to get the song order just right (what would best complement an *amuse-bouche* of grilled figs stuffed with blue cheese? "Don't Think Twice, It's All Right"? "Cyprus Avenue"?) that somehow, when it was time to open, I was still racing around with damp hair plastered to my head, in my highest heels, printing out the night's menus, ignoring the still-empty walls, the not-yet-working fireplace. Ignoring the fact that we were still without a name for the place.

Griffin was right about one part, though: being nameless wasn't a problem. Everyone in town knew exactly where to go. Everyone in the six towns over too, judging by the crowd present by 5:35 P.M., a mere five minutes after we soft-opened the door, when already there wasn't an empty seat to be found.

There was barely standing room anywhere in the entire restaurant, in fact; the overflow of friends (and friends of friends) who hadn't secured a table in the five thirty, seven thirty, or nine thirty seatings were all standing anxiously around the bar. Jesse was not yet behind it, as he had promised to be, and the lone bartender was unequal to the task of serving drinks to everyone choosing to wait, hoping that a seat would open up at one of the community tables, hoping someone they knew would walk through the big, red door with a reservation and ask them to join.

I, meanwhile, was of little help. It was my first night ever hostessing (note once again: the ill-advised choice to wear my highest heels) and instead of doing the wise thing of sending people on their way—graciously offering to make them a reservation to join us later in the week, or over the next weekend—I was busy making promises I knew I couldn't keep. Hang here for just another half hour or so. Hang here until I can figure out where I can seat you.

I was so busy offering false hope that eventually I had to sneak into the kitchen (a pile of menus still in hand) to hide from our increasingly hungry and annoyed patrons.

"Why aren't they going home?" I asked Griffin, peeking at their irritated faces through the small kitchen window. "Don't they know I'm too busy to deal with them right now?"

If Griffin weren't Griffin, this would be the moment he'd have said to me, *Seriously? I should be asking you the same thing.*

But instead, he laughed—loose and easy—as he continued plating his warm peach salad. Getting ready to move over to the entrée station, where his sous-chefs, Nikki and Dominic, were readying his beautiful branzino and herbs soaking in its parchment paper, his homemade balsamic reduction sweet enough to eat.

"It's not a big deal," Griffin said, "Just go out to the wine shack and grab a bottle of the Prosecco. Look for the Adami. The Adami's good."

"The Adami," I repeated. Then I realized: "And pour a tall glass for anyone determined to wait it out?"

He shrugged. "I was going to say, pour yourself one," he said. "But that works too."

I kissed him on the cheek, and headed toward the back door, holding it open against the wind.

"You're a genius!" I said. "And a consummate professional!"

"Be careful though," he called after me, as I stepped into the alley. "We didn't install the lights in the shack yet."

"I've got it all under control," I said. "I'll be back!"

"I'll be here," he said.

I made a beeline toward the small, wooden shack—the cold catching me anyway. And, yet, even as I wrapped my arms around myself more tightly, I couldn't help but catch a glance of the sky. It was, after all, pretty spectacular. The incredible stars and late-winter moon, lighting it up. It was like nothing I had ever seen, a sky that impossibly bright. I couldn't help but think that that felt like a good thing—like a good omen—for the restaurant. For the night ahead.

I removed the padlock and stepped up into the small shack, barely lit—only by that bright sky—and I said it out loud, *"Adami,"* reminding myself what I was looking for among the dark bottles, some still in boxes, most shelved and ready to go.

Then I spotted it out of the corner of my eye on a lower shelf—showing off its orange label, the flair of its bright green bottle. A row of Adami.

I reached down and lifted two bottles out, checking each of their labels to be certain. Which was when, from where he stood right behind me in the wine shack doorway, he spoke up.

"Hello, Adams. . . ."

Nick. Saying hello. Just like that.

I turned around fast. I turned around so fast—absolutely convinced I couldn't have heard it, what I was absolutely convinced I'd heard—that I dropped them. I dropped both of the Adamis as soon as we were face-to-face, green glass flying everywhere, the sparkly, cool liquid covering Nick's ridiculously heavy winter boots, my ridiculously open toes.

I dropped to my knees, immediately starting to search for the sharp, green shards—starting to sop up the bubbly wine. This instead of hello. This instead of, *what are you doing here?*

Nick dropped down to his knees too, right across from me, our knees almost touching.

"Careful there," he said.

I ignored him and kept picking up the shards, which made a lot of sense. Because cutting my finger open would really show him who was boss.

"Maybe we should go inside and get gloves or something?" he said. "It's a lot of glass."

"No thanks," I said. "I'm fine."

It was the first thing I said to him as though it hadn't been—*how long?*—since we'd last spoken. The first thing on the other side of our breakup. The other side of my marriage.

Nick just nodded. "Fair enough," he said.

Then he too got to work in the dark, also searching for the visible larger pieces, until he found one of the bottle's necks, its orange wrapping still intact, holding it out to me, like a present.

This was when I looked at him—first at the bottle's neck, then at him. He was dressed in a dumb Batman T-shirt beneath his blue button-down shirt. And back in his old wire-rim glasses again, like he'd never been a day without them. Looking unshaven and intent and exactly like himself. Which, is to say, absolutely perfect to me.

"I thought you were in London," I said.

"I was," he said. He pushed the wire-rims higher up on his nose. "I mean . . . I am."

"Then what are you doing here?"

"I was in the neighborhood?" he said, trying to make a joke. But his eyes looked tired behind the glasses. They looked sad to me.

And we were still on the wine shack floor. There was that. We were on the floor, looking right at each other.

I moved back, farther away from him. "I need to go inside," I said. "I'm sorry you came so far, Nick. I really am. But I need to go back inside. And you need to go. Right now."

I started to stand up, but he reached out and took my arm, gently—like it was his right—keeping me there, on my knees.

"Wait," he said. "I came a long way."

I shook my head. "No one asked you to."

"Fine. But will you just wait for one second?"

"For what?" I said.

But I knew for what. Even after so much time, I knew. It was all too familiar between us. Like we could just pick up right where we left off. This was what Nick was counting on. That love would do what it often threatened to do: remind you that it was timeless, as if that were its entire story.

Nick could ask his questions later. We could fight and talk and get nowhere later. We could figure out whether the details of the time since we parted were only details later. But if he kept me there, that close to him, his hand on my arm, his lips moving closer to my lips—if he kissed me there—he could decide that still meant something, maybe even everything.

So there I was, about to stand up, about to disengage, but not midmotion yet. I was about to be midmotion, but I wasn't yet. I was still on my knees. Because there is always a moment, between the moment when you might, and the moment when you don't.

And, in that moment, my husband walked in.

Griffin was standing in the entranceway to the wine shack—a large flashlight in his hands, his eyes fixed on Nick—as Nick and I jumped up, almost in sync, which somehow seemed like the worst possible place to start. The worst possible place for what was coming.

"Griffin . . ." I said.

"Hey there," Griffin said.

He still wasn't looking at me, though. He still wasn't looking anywhere near me, his eyes tight on the one person who should never have been in his wine shack without an invitation.

I felt the need to fix the situation, fast, but I didn't know how. *This isn't what it looks like,* I wanted to say. But it was probably somewhat what it looked like: me on the floor of Griffin's wine shack with the last person I should have been on the floor of his wine shack with—two bottles of broken wine between us, his lips making their way toward mine.

Besides, I'd heard those exact words in too many bad television shows, in too many B movies, where the exact opposite was far closer to the truth. I'd heard them from Griffin, himself, just the other day, hadn't I? He and Gia talking over coffee—a large, cumbersome bar between them. It didn't seem to be a good time to point that out, even though part of me wanted to. As if that would make us even.

So instead I dug deep to find the right thing to say.

"What are you doing out here?" I asked. "Isn't the branzino getting cold?"

Apparently, I didn't dig deep enough.

Griffin held out the flashlight for me to take—meeting my eyes, for the first time, making me wish he hadn't. "I thought you might need this," he said.

"Thank you, I do. I dropped the Adami." I turned the flashlight on, shining it at the liquid and glass all over the floor, like proof. "I dropped two of them, actually," I said. "At least it wasn't three. . . ."

Really, someone needed to shut me up.

Griffin reached out his hand toward Nick. "And you must be Nick?" he said, a little too calmly.

"It's good to meet you," Nick said.

And they shook hands. They shook hands in this weird way that I thought someone might be about to get punched. But they let go, and no one was punched. Of course no one was. We were all adults here.

"I'm really sorry to just show up like this, on such an important night," Nick said. "I didn't know your restaurant was opening tonight. Or I didn't know until my flight already landed, and the taxi dropped me at your house."

"Where did you come in from?" Griffin said.

There was no way to make London sound good. No way in the world. This was probably why Nick didn't exactly answer.

"I'm on my way to New York," he said. "For work."

Nick's eyes were on me now, but I wouldn't look at him. I was too busy looking between Griffin and the ground. The ground and Griffin. And Griffin was looking at Nick. Just at Nick. It was like musical chairs, the staring version.

"You ready for this?"

We all turned to see Jesse standing in the doorway of the increasingly crowded wine shack: Jesse, who was looking more than a little confused, and carrying a supersize bag of BAR-B-Q Fritos. Why he was munching on BAR-B-Q Fritos in the middle of his brother's restaurant opening, I had no idea.

"Cheryl's *pregnant*," Jesse said.

"What?" I said.

I flashed the flashlight right at him, right at his eyes, Jesse hurrying to cover them.

"Turn that off," Jesse said. "Don't I have enough problems?"

We all have enough problems, I thought, catching Nick's bewildered expression out of the corner of my eye.

I clicked the useless flashlight off and put it down on a shelf, away from me, just in case I felt compelled to turn it on again.

Jesse, meanwhile, was shaking his head.

"I can't even believe it. I mean, can you? I pick up the telephone tonight, and, bear in mind, this is the first time she's called in weeks without immediately asking to speak to the little guys and, I'm like, 'Hello there, *wife,*' and she was like, 'I'm not calling for small talk, I'm *pregnant,* you asshole!' Like it's my fault . . . well, in a way, I guess it is." He paused, noticing Nick. "Who is this guy?"

"Jesse," Griffin said, interrupting his brother, patting him on the back. "Come on. Let's go inside and talk about this."

"I don't want to go inside and talk about this," Jesse said. "I want to talk about this here. Where the good booze is!"

"Well, I'm going back in," Griffin said. "I have a restaurant of hungry people waiting. So if you'll excuse me . . ."

And, with that, he turned to leave.

"Griffin . . ." I said, calling after him.

Maybe I should have followed him. But all I could do was

stand there as he started through the alleyway, my heart dropping as he went. I could feel it dropping all the way down to my stomach. Just watching him go.

"What's up with him?" Jesse said, turning back to me. "I'm the one here with child. Two, apparently!"

Jesse looked crazed, even in the dark, trying unsuccessfully to get a handle on what he now knew.

"Annie, I'm so sorry about all of this," Nick said. "I really am. But if I could just have one minute alone with you before I leave . . ."

I shook my head. "No way," I said.

He looked at me, and nodded, seeing that I meant it. "Okay," he said. "I'll go."

Which might have marked it as the end—this surprise visit, this bad trip—for then at least. Except for Jesse.

"Wait . . . so who are you?" Jesse asked.

Nick was walking past him out the door. Nick this close to already being past him.

"He's going, Jesse," I said.

But Nick turned back and introduced himself. "Nick Campbell," he said. "I'm an old friend of Annie's."

Jesse nodded, starting to bring his attention back to me. Then—it was as if something occurred to him—he stopped midswitch, his eyes getting wide.

"Wait, you're Nick?" he said. "As in Annie's ex, Nick?"

But before Nick could even answer—before I could answer for him—Jesse dropped his Fritos to the ground and reached back, popping Nick hard, right in the jaw. One continuous motion, an unnatural crack, Nick flying backward and landing on the ground.

I bent down, instinctively, holding on to both of his shoulders. "Are you okay?" I asked.

Nick nodded, attempting to move his bloodied jaw around. "Yeah. I'm fine . . ." he said. "I guess I deserved that."

I looked up toward Jesse. "What the hell, Jesse?" I said. "What is that accomplishing? We *are all* adults here!"

"Didn't he just *say* he deserved it?" he said.

"Doesn't matter! We are all adults here!" I said, louder— quite clearly, on my way to completely losing it.

Jesse just shrugged and—stopping only to pick up his bag of BAR-B-Q Fritos—walked over us and out of the wine shack. Leaving me not far from where I started, alone with Nick, and somehow back on my knees.

"I want to understand what were you thinking," I said, "just showing up here?"

Nick and I were in the bathroom in the lobby of the closest local hotel—the Hotel Northampton—the closest place where I could leave him in his state. Me, using one of the hotel's ancient, monogrammed towels to blot at the blood on Nick's busted lip; Nick, sitting on the countertop before me, holding on to the back of his neck with one hand, steadying himself, holding a glass of scotch in the other—steadying himself in that way too.

"I said I was sorry," he said. "And I am. Sorry."

"Fine," I said, pulling back, studying my handiwork. "But how's that the same thing as an answer?"

He looked at me, confused. "What's the question again?"

"Nick, come on."

I tossed the towel into the small wicker basket and took a seat in the faded recliner across the small seating area, crossing my arms over my chest. It was too much to think about Griffin's restaurant opening being tainted by this. It was too unforgivable.

But there it was: an undeniable truth. And there I was with the unforgivable party.

I shook my head. "Everything's such a mess now," I said. "You made a choice. *I* made a choice."

"I know," Nick said.

I looked up at him. "Apparently you don't, or we wouldn't be here."

If I were honest, what Nick was doing here wasn't the most important question: What was *I* doing here? In a hotel lobby, nine long miles from my husband. Why hadn't I gone back into the restaurant instead?

I did. Or, I should say, I tried to. But Griffin was moving fast around the kitchen, back in his element and comfortable, clearly trying to forget what had just occurred—moving so fast, even when he saw me standing there before him. He told me we'd talk later. It seemed kinder to honor his request—to leave him be. To give him back his night, the rest of it.

And so I came here, instead, believing that in his beat-up state, Nick needed a hand. Believing also that it could be valuable, getting answers to my questions. Getting some final answers, so I could close the door. As if they existed. Final answers, closed doors.

"Can we . . . talk about something else, please?" Nick said. "For just a minute or two?"

The blood had dripped all the way down the front of his Batman T-shirt, had fallen onto his jeans. Leaving dirty, brown splotches all over the front of him. It was making him look far worse than I could ever remember seeing him look. It was making it hard to be that hard on him.

"Like what, Nick?" I said, more gently.

"Like *anything*."

He was holding up his glass of scotch now, holding it right up to his swelling chin.

Suddenly, it was too much to fight him, especially when it felt—even though it was his own fault—like he'd already lost.

I took a deep breath in.

"How's my dog doing?" I said.

"Good," he said. "Really good."

"Yeah?"

He pulled his phone out of his pocket. "I brought you some pictures, if you want to see."

I nodded. I did. It was the one thing I did want, unequivocally, right then.

So he tossed his phone across the room, I caught it, and my heart started to speed up as I scrolled through. Looking at my sweet, old Mila, napping on the windowsill in Nick's flat, walking through a Park—Battersea, I assumed—flirting with a cat by the Victoria railway station sign (yes, a cat). Like me, apparently, my girl didn't know what shouldn't be a go.

"Miss Mila . . ." I said, shaking my head in disbelief. "Who knew she was such a European?"

"Surprising, isn't it?" he said. "A little less surprising is how much she misses you."

"It's mutual," I said. "Low blow though, showing me pictures of her."

"You asked."

And he was right. I had asked. I wanted to know everything about what was going on with Mila. If I admitted it, I wanted to know more about Nick too. Nick, meanwhile, was taking a long sip of scotch, and I could see it in his eyes. That he was trying to decide whether he knew enough about what was going on with me to feel safe saying it. Whatever he'd come all this way to say.

"I've actually been living in Pimlico," he said.

I looked up at him. "What do you mean?"

He shrugged. "It felt too weird, you know?" he said. "Living in a place you picked for us. Without you there . . ."

I nodded, taking a last look at the photograph of Mila on the phone, attempting to avoid the eye contact he was trying to make. Then, still not looking, I tossed his phone back to him. Which, I like to believe, was the primary reason that the toss went short—the phone landing on the floor, beneath him, both of us staring down at it. Neither of us standing up to get it.

He took another sip of his drink.

"And the thing is, I've just been thinking for a while . . . all that time in my own place, the accidental place, and I just keep going over and over it: how we spend so much time trying to listen to each other, you know? We spend so much time rewarding ourselves for trying so hard to listen, that somehow, we can miss it . . ." He paused. "The thing the person we love most is too afraid to tell us."

I pulled my knees closer to myself, wrapping my arms around knees.

"Okay . . ." I said. "What was I too afraid to tell you, Nick?"

This was when, as an answer, he reached into his pocket—nervously, slowly—pulling something out and looking at it. Before tossing it over, across the small space between us.

It was a small red box. Not velvet. But a ring box all the same. I opened it. And, inside, saw a diamond ring. And such a pretty one—a little like it was from another time. A little like it belonged right here, with us, in this aging sitting room.

I took it out, holding it between my thumb and index finger, looking back up at him.

"I don't understand," I said.

I was still holding the ring between my fingers, still totally unsure what was going on.

"I came here tonight because I was going to propose."

"To who?" I asked.

"You."

I looked back down at the ring, the olden-days ring, completely and utterly speechless. "But . . . I'm married," I said.

"I know that."

I looked back up at him. "You waited until I was married to ask me to marry you?" I said.

He started to answer me, but I put my hand up to cut him off.

"Are you nuts?" I said.

"Just look."

He motioned for me to look inside the ring, where he'd written the same thing he'd written on the back of a locket, in another life, the one we lived in together: *For you, for always.*

"This is crazy," I said.

Then I stood up to go. Why was it taking so long to get out of this terrible room?

"Look, Annie, I know it's so screwed up between us now," he said. "And I know it's in large part my fault."

He was standing up now too, blocking my exit. Putting his hands up in the air, between us, in the calm-down motion.

"But you need to know that nothing ever happened. With Pearl," he continued. "It was never about her. It was about the idea of her, the idea of that kind of life . . . something simpler, stationary. About what I thought I was supposed to want, versus what I actually want, if that makes any sense."

"Not a lot," I said.

He looked at me, and in some ways I was waiting for an answer, but in some ways I knew exactly what he meant. And he knew that I knew. He was trying to tell me that nothing happened. What are the lines you can cross and come back from? Hadn't he stayed somewhere within the worst ones?

"We want the same things. We've built our lives, our careers, around them. And we can still have what we had, Adams. I already have two projects lined up in Europe over the next six months. And it looks like I'm going to get to shoot the new movie in Brazil at the end of the year. We can travel the world together." He smiled at me. "It was unfair of me to judge you for wanting that, for wanting that freedom. When clearly that's what I want too. What I want with you."

I tried to think of how to say no—that *that* wasn't what I wanted anymore. I wanted something more solid. Not starts and stops of a life—something more continuous, more grounded, something that could grow. But then how could I explain the part of me that had been looking for a way out of Williamsburg from the moment I arrived?

"I need to leave here, Nick," I said.

"I know what you were afraid to tell me," he said, instead of listening. "You probably don't think about it much now, but the day I left, you weren't that *surprised*. You seemed, at least a part of you seemed, to be expecting it."

"What's your point?"

"My point is, it all just got to my head, for a minute. The movie's success and my three and a half minutes of fame. It got me questioning all sorts of things about my life. And I couldn't be more sorry about how that's impacted you. I think you know that." He paused. "And, the thing is, I just keep thinking that now I know it too, now I can make it okay for you, the part that scares you the most."

"Which is what?" I said, finally.

"You can count on me," he said. "I'll always be here."

I looked at him in shock.

"I might screw up and get off track, Annie," he said. "But, if you give me a chance to, I swear I'll always make it right. . . ."

I felt something breaking open inside of me. And I had to get away from him. Not because I was mad and sad and totally pissed off. But for the part of me that wasn't. For the part of me that was something else.

"I've got to go," I said.

Then I pushed past him out the door.

I felt better immediately after I was away from him. After the heavy, old door was between us. I took a breath, let it out, and kept moving.

Except that halfway through the lobby, I felt something in my hand, and looked down to see it. The ring. I was still carrying the ring.

And the breath went back in, in a bad way. Because I had to go back into the sitting room, where I found a bloodied Batman, standing there—still and lost—exactly where I'd left him.

I didn't say, *This is yours.* I didn't say anything.

I just put the ring on the floor, right by Nick's phone, not risking handing it to him directly. Not risking any more contact.

We both looked down at the ring, resting there.

And this time, when I left, I ran.

A little before 3 A.M. I walked into the house, carrying two dripping brown bags, to find Griffin sitting at the kitchen table, still awake, still decompressing from the night. He had a large coffee mug in front of him—the pot making more on the stove—a book open on the table.

"Hey there," I said.

"Hey there," he said.

His eyes went to the brown bags, then back to me. He looked tired sitting there—not so much mad, but very tired, eerily calm and tired, which made it even harder for me to know exactly where to start.

I walked into the kitchen, gingerly taking the seat across the table from him, putting the brown bags on the table.

"When did you get home?" I asked.

He picked up his mug, one-handed, held it to his mouth. "Not too long ago," he said. "We decided to do a midnight supper for the old faithful who'd stuck it out all night."

"What did you make?"

He gave me a look, like he didn't want to answer that—like

this was, quite possibly, the last question in the world that should be asked right then. But I had a plan. Or I thought I did.

"Portobello mushroom sliders," he said. "And spicy onion soup."

"Did you have a second to eat anything yourself?" I asked.

He shook his head, his hand still wrapped tightly around his mug.

"Not really," he said.

"Well that's good. Because . . ."

I reached into one of the bags and pulled it out: a perfect red Lasse's lobster claw—the one Griffin had told me about that first night. The Lasse's lobster claw that he'd promised me that night, on the other side of the country, in that first minute where we were learning to promise things to each other. It felt like something—maybe not enough, but something—if I could deliver that promise to him now.

"I thought I could make you some eggs," I said.

He reached over and took the claw from my hand. "You went all the way up to Lasse's?" he said.

I nodded. "In the middle of the night," I said.

"How did you get him to serve you?"

I shrugged. "I have magical powers."

He nodded, putting the claw back in the bag.

"No arguments here," he said. "That was sweet of you. Thank you."

"You're welcome," I said, smiling, like it was no big deal. It fact, it had been a fairly exhausting ordeal that ended with me begging Lasse for a few small claws, being forced to barter them for several items I had no idea how I'd get my hands on, including a first edition copy of my newspaper and a Jack Nicholson autograph.

I stood up, and headed toward the stove, firing it up. "So what do you say?" I asked. "Can I make you some eggs?"

"Annie, you don't have to do that."

"Are you kidding me?" I said. "I want to. I'm starving too. I mean, it goes without saying that they may not turn out as good as yours did, but you never know, right? I do have the magical claws on my side."

This was when I opened the refrigerator, and saw what I didn't have on my side, what it turned out was missing. Maybe the most obvious thing. The eggs.

"We have no eggs?" I said.

Griffin smiled. "We'll do it tomorrow."

It was too much. I sat down, depleted, my head falling into my hands.

"Who has no eggs?" I asked. "And do we know anyone who can put us in touch with Jack Nicholson?"

He looked at me, confused, and then reached over and put his hand on my arm, calming me. "It's okay," he said.

I shook my head. "You don't understand," I said. "I wanted to do one thing right. I thought if I could do one thing right . . ."

"You do a lot of things right," he said.

"But I ruined your night, or Nick ruined it. And I couldn't stop that." I looked right at him. "I am so sorry about that, Griffin. I'm so sorry. You have no idea how much I want to make it okay."

"I have an idea."

"You do?" I said. "So you're not mad?"

He gave me a look, just a flash, which let me know he was. Then he looked back at his coffee mug, which was getting dangerously close to empty.

"*Mad* might not be the right word," he said.

"What is, then?"

Griffin walked over to the stove, and started to pour himself some more coffee—reaching in the cupboard to get another mug, and bring some over to me too.

"Michael from your paper came in after you left," he said.

"Who?" I asked, it taking me a minute to connect the dots—the many Michaels I knew at work, until I could picture him: a small guy, originally from Martha's Vineyard, who wrote the "Wine & Spirits" column. "Michael Thomas?" I said. "The wine critic?"

He nodded, taking his seat again, handing over my mug.

"He was visiting his daughter at Smith College. Thought he'd check out the restaurant, see if he could find an angle to write about it." He paused, putting his coffee mug to his lips. "He asked me to congratulate you on your promotion."

I looked up at him, but he wasn't meeting my eyes.

"They offered you a job in London?"

"Yes," I said. "Well . . . based out of London."

"When?" he said. "Not that it matters, exactly, but when did they let you know about the offer?"

I started talking entirely too quickly, trying to explain. "Griffin, I was going to talk to you about it," I said. "But with the restaurant opening and everything else that's been happening around here, I just haven't had a chance yet, and since I'm not going, obviously . . ."

"To London? Where Nick is?"

"Based out of London," I mumbled, as though this was the point. "And Nick's not there for much longer."

"So do you think you want it?" he asked.

For a second, I didn't know if he was talking about Nick or the job—my eyes getting wide.

"The job?" he said, looking more than a little irritated.

I shook my head. "No, I don't."

He looked right at me, the coffee still by his mouth, waiting for something closer to the truth.

"I don't know, Griffin," I said. "I don't really know anymore. But I am worried about what else I'm going to do here. What else I can *do*. That's not a secret."

I looked back up at Griffin, who was still silent. But I wondered if he was hearing the rest of what I was thinking: about seeing Nick, about what that was triggering for me. Because instead of getting madder, it was like it just washed his anger away. And he gave me a smile I didn't recognize.

"What?" I asked.

He shook his head. "Before you walked in the door tonight, I was just thinking how my mother used to take Jesse and me to the General Store on Friday afternoons, back when we were little kids. She'd do her shopping for the weekend, and we'd each get to pick one candy," he said. "Just one. And, the thing was, Jesse would always know exactly which candy he wanted. These hard little guys called Pop Rocks."

I watched him reach over, put the brown bags from Lasse's in the refrigerator, move them away from us.

"I remember Pop Rocks," I said. "Wasn't that the candy they said could kill you if you ate it with a soda? The one that they say killed that kid Mikey from the Life cereal commercial?"

"Exactly," he said. "And I don't think they actually killed him."

I shook my head. "Man, those were great."

"That's the thing," he said. "Jesse would grab the candy and be out of the store in fifteen seconds flat. And I'd still be standing there, just staring at the candy shelf for as long as my mother shopped. They'd play these old records in the store . . . the Beatles. The Beach Boys. Billie Holiday. So my mother thought I wanted to listen to the music, but really I couldn't decide. I'd pick up something pretty great, put it back down, pick up something else. And just when Emily would call out that I was out of time, Jesse screaming through the window for me just to get some more Pop Rocks, I'd panic, as only a six-year-old can, and end up picking something pretty awful."

"Like Fun Dip?"

"On several occasions, yes."

"That's the saddest thing I've ever heard," I said.

He smiled, giving me a small laugh. Then he looked right at me.

"You shouldn't take that job, Annie," he said, solid and firm.

"And I'm not saying that because of me. Or because it'd be difficult to go with you. I would figure out how to, if I thought it was the right thing. For you, for us."

"Then why are you saying it?"

He shrugged. "Because I'm worried you've just convinced yourself you need to go there, and that's not the same thing as actually wanting to."

"I don't follow," I said.

He paused. "You were the one that told me you wanted a different life."

"Well, I'm not sure my *different* life is entirely realistic," I said.

"Says who?"

"Says hundreds of ruined photographs," I said. "Says me not knowing what I'd do with them even if they weren't. Says this travel column, my spending so much time on the road, all of it being the only life I've ever known."

He looked at me, not as if this was completely unclear, but as if this type of clarity wasn't of much use to him. It made me feel lonely, especially after feeling understood again just a few hours before by someone who shouldn't be understanding me at all anymore.

"I can't just become someone else, Griffin," I said, trying again.

"Who's talking about you becoming someone else?" he said. "I'm talking about you becoming more like yourself."

I leaned back, away from him. *More like myself.* This was the worst part. I didn't know why I couldn't get there.

"That's the thing," he said. "That's why I started thinking about the Pop Rocks story. I used to be so frustrated that Jesse knew exactly what he wanted. That he could just be happy with it . . . really content. I never thought I'd be built that way. And then it changed."

"When?" I asked.

He gave me a smile. "When did we meet, again?"

I smiled back, and then looked down. "That's not true," I said.

"No, not exactly," Griffin said. "But that's not what I'm saying anyway. I'm saying it took a long time to figure out it wasn't about me finding my version of Pop Rocks."

"What was it about?"

He stood up, taking his mug with him. "It was about learning to leave the store before time was up," he said.

Then he leaned down, for one more second, to kiss me on the cheek. Like that was something we did.

"Take the job, Annie," he said, into my ear. "Go to London."

I looked up as he pulled back, moving away from me.

"I don't understand," I said. "Didn't you just say that I shouldn't go? Didn't you just get finished saying that?"

He tilted his head, met my eyes. "I just keep wondering, what made Nick think he could just show up here?" he said. "Was that about him, or was it about you?"

I didn't know how to answer that, which seemed to be the only answer Griffin needed.

Part of me wanted to scream out, *It isn't about Nick*. But the words wouldn't come. Because there was another part of me that looked at that antique ring a second too long—that listened to Nick's offer a second too long—to know that Nick wasn't factoring into my confusion. And then, there was the biggest part of me: the part that didn't think this was about wanting Nick again, at all. But that couldn't ignore what seeing him made abundantly clear. That I was no closer to being present here. That part of me still craving an exit strategy.

"I don't know how to explain it, Griffin. I woke up one day and it's like I'd ended up in a completely new life. I know I chose that, but it doesn't feel that simple," I said. "None of it feels simple to me."

He was already on his way toward the door, he was already on his way away from me. And this wasn't enough to keep him.

"I can't fix that for you, Annie," he said. "I don't want to spend my life trying to."

He looked at me for one last second. He didn't look angry, or upset. He looked clear, certain.

Then he was gone.

The next morning I called Peter.

"I think I may have screwed everything up . . ." I said.

I was standing in the kitchen, the house quiet—perfectly peaceful—the first bit of sun hovering over the backyard, over the forest, making the trees shine.

I turned away from the window.

"Peter," I said, "don't be mad, but what if I said I think you may be right and I do need to go? To London, I mean?"

The words felt weird on my tongue, waxlike and wrong. Yet, I was able to ignore that—had to ignore that—because I also felt a certain kind of relief, just hearing them, out in the world, ready to do their work.

"My love," he said. His voice was still husky with sleep. "I'd tell you that you could have waited until seven A.M. to share with me what I already know. It's seven A.M. for unsurprising news. That is the rule."

"So it's not too late to take the job?" I asked.

"Of course it isn't too late," he said. "I accepted the position on your behalf last week."

I looked down at the phone, totally confused. "But how could you do that?" I asked.

"Well, easily," he said. "Melinda Beckett Martin, the paper's deputy managing editor, not to mention Caleb Beckett the First's very favorite niece, called to ask me if you were taking the job, and I told her of course you were. That you couldn't wait to bring 'Checking Out' into international syndication. That despite appearances to the contrary, you weren't *a fool.*"

"No, but what I'm saying is . . ."

I looked around the kitchen, the twins' stuff strewn about, Cheryl's watering can left by the sink; pictured Griffin sleeping upstairs; thought again of all that I was walking away from in the name of not being sure if I had gotten there for the right reasons. And how I could stay.

"How did you know I'd get here?" I asked.

He sighed. Then he sighed again, just in case I missed it.

"My love, how can I say this gently before hanging up on you and going back to sleep?" he said. "I never thought you weren't going to get here."

. . . .

I don't remember how it happened, exactly—who suggested it first—that we go for a walk. It didn't matter. Both of us, I think, already knew what was about to happen, and neither of us wanted to be inside of the house when it did.

It was after midnight, the moon steering us away from town— toward farther-off farmland, toward the mountains themselves.

I wasn't sure what to start by saying, but it felt wrong to make him do it. It felt wrong to do anything but make this as painless as possible. As if, for either of us, that was a possibility.

"Do you remember the conversation we had at the beach that day?" I said. "How I tried to tell you about the best and worst thing about being with Nick? And I said the worst was that I rarely remembered feeling safe?"

"Sure . . ."

"I think that it wasn't fair to put that on him. That feeling of safe? I'm not sure I've ever felt that. And maybe instead of just deciding that Nick was the problem, or the latest in a series of problems, I should have thought about something else."

"Which is what?"

I shrugged. "Maybe I'm the problem," I said.

Griffin looked at me. "Maybe he just wasn't the right person."

"And what's the excuse this time?" I said. "The evidence is mounting that I don't have any idea how to do it, Griffin. Make a home with someone else, feel comfortable in it. And maybe I won't be able to figure out how, unless I can do that first piece on my own. Make myself safe and comfortable. And then be able to feel like I'm choosing into everything else."

It wasn't exactly what I wanted to say. But it was close enough. It was close enough for Griffin to understand.

He leaned in and put his arms around me.

"I know it sounds crazy. How can someone figure out how to stay by going again?" I said, trying to explain it. "But going again is the only way I've ever found what I'm looking for."

He was still holding me there, to him, when he spoke, so I couldn't see his face.

"I'm not sure we get to, Annie," he said. "I'm not sure we get to choose when or where we find what we're looking for."

I started to say that maybe that was true, maybe our timing was the problem, maybe if we met five years from now, or five months, or five minutes even, but—and I was looking for the *but,* for the way out—I was scared he was saying what he was saying to convince me to stay. To stay right where I was, with him, and try harder.

But then I looked up at him, into his strong and resolved face, and realized he was saying it to let me go.

Which was when he kissed me, one last time. And did.

A few years after I started "Checking Out," there was a brief
period when we expanded the column to include a supple-
ment called "Late Checkout," which focused on finding
the best deals or free activity alternatives in any city you happened
to be visiting. In Montreal, for example, "Late" would recommend
that instead of paying for a guided dinner-and-dancing boat tour of
the St. Lawrence River, you should consider heading down to the
ferry on the Jacques-Cartier Pier, which provided visitors with gorgeous views of Montreal's downtown, and a great way to visit the
old fort at Musée David M. Stewart. All for a fraction of the cost.

But "Late" failed, monumentally and fast, which came as a
surprise to me. It had been my idea, and I had thought it was a
good one. Who didn't want to experience a city without breaking
the bank? It wasn't until years later that I realized what we had
done wrong. It wasn't that we provided a free option, it was that
we had also provided the *expensive* option beside it. It was in
the comparison that we lost the readers. Because all they could
see, then, was the option they wouldn't be taking. All they could
think about was what they'd get if they could spend more. About
what was about to be missed.

I arrived in London late on a Sunday afternoon—stepping onto the tarmac at Heathrow Airport some seventeen hours before I was scheduled to report to my new office at Buckingham Gate.

For my second major move in less than a year, I'd taken very little with me. Two suitcases, two pictures of Mila, and the phone numbers of two people I knew in the entire country— one number was my new boss's, Melinda Martin. The other I couldn't feel good about dialing. Not yet.

The newspaper sent a car service to the airport to fetch me, which provided a far nicer introduction to my new hometown than the Tube would have granted. As a bonus, the sun had started setting over Central London as the driver, Thomas, took the long way to my new abode, pointing out the sites he thought I'd enjoy along the way: Trafalgar Square and Nelson's Column; the National Gallery and Buckingham Palace; Waterloo Bridge and Piccadilly Circus. I didn't have the heart to tell him that I'd been to all of those places before for "Checking Out." I didn't ever want to have that kind of heart.

He smiled at me in the rearview mirror. "So what kind of writing do you do for the newspaper?" he asked me.

I shrugged. "Mostly," I said, "obituaries."

Thomas took a right down Sloane Street, and I looked out the window at the hustle and bustle of late-day shoppers hur- rying in for a chance at final sales, at early-evening restaurant- goers, filling up the good window seats while they still could. Then Thomas hooked a left onto a tiny side street, which looked like, and felt like, an entirely different world. An exceptionally peaceful and intimate one, with just a handful of manicured gardens and small, beautiful buildings greeting me.

"This is lovely," I said.

"It's the best block in London," he said. "Truly. There have been books written about it."

"I believe it," I said.

Thomas shut off the ignition, and turned toward me. "And it's your home," he said, giving me a bright smile.

I tried to look as happy about that as he did. *You're choosing this,* I reminded myself. You're doing the right thing. Or, at least, the only thing.

And thankfully, as we walked into my new flat together—each carrying a suitcase—I didn't have to try so hard anymore to believe it. It was, hands down, the single most charming apartment I'd ever seen. It looked like a carriage house, with large windows and tall, white pillars, an old-fashioned kitchen (complete with a farmer's sink), and rustic wood furniture running through the hallways and leading up a tiny staircase to the loveliest bedroom. The river just outside every window, endless, and glowing.

"Quite the digs they've handed you here," Thomas said, as we stood by the living room windows, filling out the paperwork he needed completed.

"It's like a ready-made life," he said.

I looked up at him, that phrase catching me. *A ready-made life.*

Then I forced a smile. And followed his eyes outside. First toward the river, then toward what was across it: Battersea. My supposed-to-be home was over there, somewhere, the one I'd picked out for Nick and me. And there I was—able to look straight at it, from a short distance. Just a few months later than planned. Didn't that mean something? That, after everything, this was where I was supposed to be?

I quickly signed along the necessary *X*'s.

"You should count yourself as lucky. I've seen some of the other places they put the newbies to stay," Thomas said. "You must be good at writing about dead people."

"Very," I heard someone say.

We turned to find Peter in the kitchen doorway, holding a bottle of Dom Perignon and two champagne flutes.

"Peter!" I said. "How did you get in here?"

"I hid in the kitchen pantry," he said. "A woman living alone? You really should check all doors upon entering."

I ran over to him, giving him a hug. And holding on, probably for a little too long. Okay, definitely for too long, Peter utilizing the expensive champagne bottle to separate us.

"Hold it together, my love," he said.

"I just can't believe it's you," I said. "What are you even doing here?"

"I told you they were sending me over here for a spell. So here I am to greet you . . ." he said. "Midspell."

I gave him a big smile. "I'm so glad to see you," I said. "I'm just so, so glad."

As I went in for another hug, tears springing to my eyes, he handed me my champagne flute.

"I thought we just decided you were going to hold it together," he said. "Let's go ahead and stick to the plan."

....

That night, wine gift in hand, Peter and I went to a cocktail party in South Kensington at the house of my new boss, Melinda Beckett Martin.

Peter had told me only a few details about Melinda, which was why I wasn't sure what to expect upon meeting her. She was *just* your typical, major success: in her midthirties, married to an Oxford professor, and *an integral part of Beckett Media*, as Peter explained, having run television programming for the company in Australia and Asia, and sending profits through the roof in both places.

But even if Peter had provided all possible details about Melinda, I'm not sure it would have adequately prepared me for what was waiting when we approached her beautiful, double-fronted Victorian home. When the door opened, Melinda herself was standing there to greet us. I reached out to hand her the bottle of wine that we'd brought.

This was my first mistake. I narrowly avoided jamming her right in the boobs with it.

I looked up—all the way up—to see a six-foot-five-inch woman, dressed in a fashionable burnt orange polka-dot skirt and white ballet slippers. Wearing just about the warmest smile I'd ever seen.

"Mr. Shepherd!" she said to Peter, in a ravishing Australian accent. "Welcome! Welcome!"

She was carrying a tray of mixed hors d'oeuvres, which she immediately moved out of the way in order to lean down and double-cheek kiss him.

Then she turned to me.

"And you must be the divine Ms. Adams that I've heard so much about?"

"That would be me," I said. "It is nice to meet . . ."

But before I could even say *you,* she was double-kissing me too and wrapping her arm around my shoulder, like we were the oldest of friends.

"We have so much to talk about," she said.

And then she was leading us through a central tiled hall into her home—a *lived-in* home, to use a Britishism: decorated with an enormous farmer's table, and photographs everywhere (wedding photos and family photos, photos of her husband and her traveling, photos from their respective childhoods), and the type of warm, playful furniture and artwork that made a home feel filled with people and music and laughter, even when it wasn't.

Now it was filled to the brim with all three. As Peter situated himself with an old friend of his from university, right by the open bar, Melinda took me around and introduced me to seemingly every single person there: my future colleagues and their drunk significant others; Melinda's neighbors and favorite friends; her *future* nanny.

She kept feeding me the delicious appetizers from her tray as we moved along through the crowd. And by the time we curled into two purple velvet chairs in the corner of the living room, the model-tall Melinda managing to do so far more gracefully than me—curling her lanky body beneath her, wrapping her hand behind her neck in rest position—I kind of loved her a little.

"So," she said, "let me start by saying thank you for that."

"For what?" I said.

"Saving me from having to think about what on earth to talk to all those people about, all on my own," she said. Then she leaned in closer, and gave me a wink. "I dread cocktail parties."

"I'm with you," I said.

"Well, we will begin with the work stuff tomorrow, but I just wanted to welcome you into the fold officially," she said. "I hear my cousin Caleb has been less than welcoming, officially or otherwise."

I shook my head. "No, I wouldn't say that," I said. "I just . . . haven't spoken to him yet."

"Well, with any luck, we'll figure out how to keep it that way for a while," she said. "He is one of those people who thinks he has all the answers. So just to piss him off, I send him e-mails marked urgent at least twice a day, asking him impossible questions, like, what is the price of a quart of milk in Adyar, India?"

I started to laugh, just as someone called Melinda's name.

"The problem is," she said, "he always knows the answer. What is worse than that?"

"Very little," I said.

She pointed at the name-caller to give her a minute. And gave me a kind look.

"I'm so sorry to leave you. But I think I have to put out a fire in the southwest corner." She circled her hands around her mouth, making a clock. "Three o'clock."

I turned to see a couple of some sort looking desperately awkward trying to talk to each other. Or desperately awkward standing together and not talking to each other. Their eyes on the floor.

"No, of course, of course . . ." I said. "Thank you for giving me as much time as you did."

She stood up again, towering over me in an embarrassing way. "It's wonderful to meet you, Annie Adams," she said.

"You too, Melinda," I said.

Then she handled me a final crab cake and ran off.

I watched her go, her bright polka dots moving away with her, and started to look around for Peter, to let him know I was ready to leave. But just then my phone rang, BLOCKED coming up on the caller ID.

Griffin, I thought immediately, and hopefully. We hadn't talked since I'd left the house earlier in the week—heading first to New York, and then to London. We hadn't talked since we had really talked. And I knew it had to come down to me, reaching out to him, if that was what I wanted. And I knew I didn't have forever to do it. I had far less than forever if I were going to turn things around. Still, I found myself hoping. But it wasn't Griffin on the other end.

It was Jordan.

"Are you still mad at me?" she asked. "And, before you answer that, please note that I've made a list of several very *compelling* reasons why you shouldn't be. Almost like an ode to my favorite column. That's number one, actually. That 'Checking Out' *is* my favorite column." She paused. "And I've written more letters to the editor than anyone on earth to say so."

I stepped out onto the balcony, where I could get some peace and quiet, the party still visible—like a silent film, before me— through the glass doors.

I sighed. "What's the point of being mad now?" I said. "It feels like a lot of energy."

"Really?" she said. "That's great news!"

"I'm glad you're pleased."

"You have no idea."

"But I do reserve the right to be mad again, when I'm feeling more up to it. And less jet-lagged."

"Reserved!" she said. "So, tell me, how is it?"

I looked at the festive party happening before me, and then turned to stare up at the starry sky above, the dry wind feeling nice against my skin.

"Unseasonably mild," I said.

"That's a good sign!" she said. "That's a very good sign! And you start this week?"

"First thing tomorrow."

I spotted Melinda through the window, which wasn't hard to do. She was doing a little tap dance for a group of guests—a chocolate layer cake in her hands, the guests applauding wildly. Whether it was for her or for the cake wasn't entirely clear.

"My new boss seems pretty great, actually," I said.

"That's the spirit!"

"Is it?"

"Yes! It's *good*, Annie, it's *right*. . . ." She paused. "And have you seen Nick yet? You know he's still there."

I almost hung up the phone, right there. "You're fired," I said.

"Okay, okay. I take it back," she said. "I'm sorry. I shouldn't have asked. It doesn't matter. You'll call him, you won't call him. I'm just glad it's all coming together out there in the world."

Through the window, I saw Melinda still tapping away, holding the cake high above her head now, moving it up and down in quick succession. Then I looked around the room at everyone else: Peter and the other editors, Melinda's many friendly friends. The nice greetings they'd all given me.

And I couldn't help but think of what Thomas the driver had said, just a few hours earlier, the two of us standing by my new living room window.

"It's a ready-made life," I said.

"Who couldn't use a ready-made life?" Jordan said. "Nothing wrong with that, at all."

The next day—more than a bit hopped up on a third cup of coffee, the jet lag having reached its full force—I found myself at my new desk in the crowded newsroom of Beckett Media's print headquarters. I had, at most, ten square feet of cubicle real estate, but it was *good* real estate: a big-windowed corner looking out at Buckingham Gate, at the Hong Kong Association and Society, their beautiful gardens, the boats in the river beyond them.

I was trying to lay out a plan of attack for my first new column—something exciting and something new—when I gave up and turned to the window, drawn to the river, feeling content staring at it. Or maybe *content* wasn't the right word. Maybe it was closer to lonely, which at least felt more honest.

Then I heard someone slide by my desk, giving its side a soft knock, pulling me out of my reverie. I looked up to find Melinda staring down at me in a slightly different polka-dot skirt than she'd been wearing the night before—and I do mean slightly: this one more cherry red than burnt orange, if someone were looking closely enough. Which, apparently, I was.

"Good skirt," I said.

"Good taste!" she said. "So, what do you think of your new space? I had to move someone from Architecture to get you the corner with the views." She paused. "That's a bit ironic, actually, isn't it?"

I smiled. "It's great," I said. "Thank you."

"Great! So, Annie girl . . ." she said. "Does anyone call you Annie girl?"

I shrugged. "My mother, maybe," I said. "When I was six."

"Well, I don't want to bring that memory back," she said.

"Probably for the best."

Then she tossed down—from her station, up closer to the sky—a Montblanc pen and a yellow legal pad, which, by some small miracle, I managed to catch.

"Walk with me," she said.

We headed down the hall, Melinda moving at a rapid pace, me moving at an even more rapid one, trying to keep up with those legs.

"Well, when I finally got the last hanger-on out my door last night," she said, "I read all of your columns over. . . ."

"All of them?"

She gently linked her arm through mine, which should have been hard to do considering our height discrepancy, but she managed it beautifully.

"Every single one, Annie," she said. "And I can honestly say I'm a fan now. We are going to have a lot of fun with the column's evolution. I am swimming with ideas."

"That's so nice to hear."

She smiled down at me. "I was struck, though, that perhaps you have a bigger story to tell about all the places you've been," she said. "Especially after so many. I feel like we need to think outside the box to figure out the right formula. To make the column feel bigger, more universally bonding."

"You think so?" I said.

"I do."

I felt myself—in spite of myself—start to get a little excited, a smile breaking out on my face. I almost started to tell her right then about my photographs—about all those homes, waiting to have their stories told. But then I stopped myself, remembering that they'd been lost. Remembering how. Remembering, also, what was lost along with them. The twins, Jesse, Williamsburg. Griffin. All of it quickly becoming a mirage, becoming a world I didn't know anymore.

"You look like you're having a thought parade over there," she said. "What's happening?"

"No no no." I shook my head. "It's nothing."

"Well, if it ever is something . . ." She gave me that big smile again. "Just know that I'm open to all ideas. I know people say that, but it's true in my case. Bad ones, good ones. Especially good ones."

I smiled.

"And, while you're thinking, what I'm looking for, primarily, is a way to simplify the column so we can brand it. Get more of you. You know what I'm asking?"

"If I say maybe, is that bad?"

She laughed, throwing her head back. "I'm not making a lot of sense yet, but just keep your thinking cap on," she said.

"I can do that," I said.

"Good," she said, unlinking her arm from mine as we approached the conference room. "Big changes are coming. Great ones."

Then with a wink, she disappeared into the conference room—me catching just a peek of Peter before the door shut.

I looked down at the legal pad. On top she had written *Annie Girl* = **World Travel Connoisseur.**

Below that, all over the page, she'd mapped out several divisions of Beckett Media: television shows related to travel, their radio programs, their Web sites. Putting them all in one large circle, *Annie Girl* written in the center, again—in the bull's-eye.

I, apparently, hadn't written anything.

. . . .

The next Friday evening, in celebration of my first full week, Peter and I decided to see a play on the West End. To go out for a late meal, afterward, at a noodle place he loved.

But we had only just gotten in a taxicab when the night felt a little ruined. I got a message on my phone that I had a new e-mail. My heart was beating as I opened my phone, hoping against hope that it was going to be some word from Griffin. As more time went by, I got more and more worried that word from him was never coming. What did I want him to say, anyway? Anything, was the answer. Anything at all. But why was I surprised that something from Griffin wasn't what was waiting for me. Something from Nick was.

This was what he wrote:

```
A-

This isn't to put any pressure on you.
Just to let you know I'm thinking of you.
Not just when you're in Massachusetts and
married. Not just when I'm not supposed to
be. In case you thought that was what this
was about. The chase. It's not. It's about
everything else.

    I'm supposed to leave London a week from
Monday. I hope to see you before then.

    I hope to have a reason not to leave,
at all.

                              Yours,

                              N.
```

"*Good* e-mail, no?" Peter said.

I turned to find him leaning over my shoulder, reading for himself.

"Peter!" I said.

"Oh, right!" he said. "Like now is a good time to start playing the role of bashful."

"*Anyway*," I said. "It doesn't matter."

"Why not?"

I shrugged. "I don't know that I can put it into words."

Peter patted my hand. "There's my star writer," he said.

"It's just that Nick says he wants to give me what I want," I said. "He wants a chance to do that now."

"And what's the problem?"

The problem was that I wasn't just angry with Nick for leaving and putting us in such a difficult place then, or even for walking back into my life when he shouldn't have and putting me in such a tricky place now. If I was being honest with myself, it was more that I had started to wonder if what Nick was offering me was less *what I want*, and more what I want*ed*. Past tense.

"The thing is," I said, "I'm not sure I'm clear on want I want anymore."

"If you're waiting to be clear on that, you may be waiting forever."

"Gee. That's comforting."

He squeezed my hand.

"Why not just give it another chance? I've always liked Nick."

I gave Peter a look, surprised somehow—and not—for that to be what came out of his mouth.

"Peter, you've never *met* Nick."

"That's *why* I like him."

"That makes no sense."

He scrunched up his nose. "Since you married Griffin, you've been so preoccupied. You haven't even wanted to travel," he said. "With Nick, you had freedom."

Freedom. There was that word again. I had organized my life to hold on to it, hadn't I? Everyone seemed to think so. Everyone—myself included—seemed to think I needed the possibility of going anywhere at any time, of infinite openness. But I was starting to wonder if maybe I had missed what freedom really looked like. Maybe it had less to do with always having a way out. Maybe it had something more to do with finding the way deeper in.

"So this is about you?" I said. "What you want for me?"

"No, it's about what you want for you." He paused. "I'm only saying that he's just your first husband. He certainly doesn't have to be your last!"

With that, Peter turned to look out the taxi window, apparently done with this conversation.

"That's a lovely exit line," I said, sarcastically.

"Look, love, sue me if you must, but that's how I feel. I just think that you and Griffin . . . the whole thing just seems complicated."

"Define complicated." I said.

"'Confusing, messy. A lot to take on,'" he said. "'Often difficult to analyze, understand, or explain.'"

I felt my chest constrict, start to close down, just discussing Griffin. Maybe because I couldn't make sense of all of it yet. When I had been in Massachusetts, I had felt overwhelmed and unsettled. So why, all the way across the world, was I feeling something else so intensely? A feeling I didn't even know before that moment, not in just that way. I was, undeniably, homesick.

"And, really," Peter continued, "no need to be angry with me just because you want to see him."

I drilled him with a look. "I don't want to see him," I said. "Wait . . . which one are you talking about?"

"You know which one I'm talking about," Peter said.

"Not really."

He squeezed my hand. "It's obvious," he said.

After the play that night, I couldn't fall asleep.

This was what I was up against: one job firing, one botched restaurant opening, a marriage proposal from someone else. No trips to speak of, no big birthdays, one awkward meeting each with the other's parents. A cold, windy, small town. Where I had no obvious job prospects. No obvious future. Where I had a crazy brother-in-law and a full house of mother-missing twin boys and five *hundred* ruined photographs. Where it was too cold to walk outside after 5:00 P.M., where it was too noisy to be inside anytime before that. Where my husband (if he still thought of himself that way) had a beautiful, homespun ex-girlfriend, a mother who didn't like me in the least, and a new, nameless restaurant in the middle of our lives, locking us in there. Locking us into the immeasurable quiet, where I could hear all of my fears that I'd chosen a life on impulse. All of my fears that I'd forever remember the one guy I'd always thought would be my answer. That one love now offering me everything. For the first time.

And this. And this too. A growing sense that maybe just once in this life someone loves us for the us we don't even know how to be yet. And if we lose him too early—in the name of all the promises in the world: a new job, a new city, an old love offering us happily ever after—we may just lose that chance to be our best self.

The next Sunday, the night before Nick was scheduled to leave London for good, I went for a late-night walk around my neighborhood, dressed in a pair of sweatpants that didn't belong outside the house. My Massachusetts coat with the rhine-stone hearts keeping me warm against the rain. Despite the wet, I ended up walking for so long that I left my neighborhood alto-gether, heading east—not admitting to myself that I was walking in the direction of Victoria station, closer to where I might run into Nick, closer to where he was living. I walked until I actually wound up in Pimlico, in front of a popular gastropub called the Orange.

I wasn't planning on going in anywhere—on my flashy hearts making a public appearance—but even though the Orange was crowded, I went inside, and found a seat at the end of the bar, right near the piano, an older couple miraculously getting up to go just as I was getting there.

As I swept into the man's seat before I lost it, the barkeep walked over and wiped down the counter in front of me, trying a little too hard not to take in my ensemble, not to stare at my rhinestone hearts.

What she didn't know was that I had no choice but to leave it on. Underneath was a kitschy T-shirt from Niagara Falls with little rainbows all over it and I FELL FOR THE FALLS written in blue. I'd picked it up during an early travel reporting gig. It made the rhinestones look like haute couture.

"What would you like?" she asked, above the noise.

I took a quick glance at the menu—trying not to remember that I'd had a full dinner a few hours before.

"I'll take a double order of the rosemary fried potatoes," I said. "And whatever you'd recommend to drink. Your call."

"I make a good basil martini," she said.

I smiled. "Anything but that," I said. "And maybe add some bourbon and extra salt?"

She smiled back. "Coming right up," she said.

The older couple had left a copy of the *Guardian* on the bar, and, as I waited for my drink, I started reading, not noticing that someone was standing over the empty seat. The older woman's.

"You probably should've gone for the basil martini," he said, his accent undeniably American.

It was so loud in there—bass music blasting, people shouting to hear each other—that for a second I thought that it was Nick. Nick, whom I had picked up the phone to call a half-dozen times, each time changing my mind before all the numbers were entered. Each time feeling like his answering wasn't going to give me the answer I was looking for. The battle between Nick and Griffin, Griffin and Nick, feeling like something else. Something that had more to do with something in me. And still, my heart picked up at the thought that Nick was standing there, which I could have taken as some sort of message from the universe, from the masters of fate. (Forgetting the fact that I helped them out by moving myself directly to the most popular pub in his neighborhood.)

But fate was offering me something else entirely.

I looked up to see the man was carrying a full basil martini in one hand—and a briefcase and another copy of the *Guardian* in the other. He couldn't have been more than thirty, despite his attire—a suit and tie that would probably cost me a month's salary, newly shined shoes. Wire-rim glasses that looked eerily similar to Nick's. And there was no denying he was handsome—in a movie-star way—tall, with a strong smile, a matching strong chin.

And from the way he threw his briefcase on the bar and sat right down next to me—sans the courtesy ask—I was guessing there was no denying that to himself either.

"I'm sure I'll be good with whatever they're bringing me," I said. "But thank you."

Just then the barkeep came back carrying a martini glass full of bright orange liquid, an even brighter yellow umbrella sticking out the side. I looked back toward Mr. Suit, who was casually moving his martini my way, and motioning to the barkeep for a new one.

"Just go for it," the man said. "I haven't even had a sip yet. It can be my rental cost."

"Rental cost?"

"For the seat."

I gave him a smile and took the martini, just as a second one was getting delivered to him.

"Thank you, that's very nice of you," I said.

He clinked his martini glass to mine. "Enjoy, then," he said. "Cheers."

He looked down at his newspaper, which I thought meant we were done with the niceties, and that I could return to mine. But then, eyes still on his paper, he started talking again.

"How long have you been an expat?" he asked.

"Not long," I said.

"How not long?"

I looked over at him, trying to decide how much I didn't feel like answering. Whether it involved my moving seats or just giving a clipped response. What about my sequins suggested I wanted company?

"A little less than a month," I said.

"What brought you here?"

Now he was looking back up, right at me. I took a sip of my drink, tried to shake myself into it. Friendliness. Reminding myself that I lived here now.

"Work," I said. "You?"

He shrugged. "Forty-two percent work, fifty-eight percent personal," he said. "Approximately."

"Just approximately?"

"I'm excellent with percentages," he said.

I smiled and went back to the paper, turning the page to the national news.

"So when I saw you at Melinda's party . . ." He pointed toward the ceiling, as if doing the math, figuring out the percentages on that. "It must have been right when you arrived, yes?"

I looked up at him, confused. "Excuse me?"

"Melinda Martin. You work for the newspaper, I assume." He pointed down at my copy of the *Guardian*. "I won't tell."

"Who are you?"

He reached out to shake my hand. "My friends call me Aly," he said. "I was going to try and talk to you that night, but you were outside on your telephone. And you looked pretty miserable. Even more miserable than now."

"At least I'm improving," I said.

"Exactly," he said.

I shook his hand. "What do you do for the paper?"

"Nothing. I'm an environmental lawyer, actually. For the good side though," he said. "You know, the misunderstood corporations."

I laughed, picking up my drink. "Making the world a better place?"

"Doing my share."

"What were you doing at the party, then?"

"My wife works for the newspaper." He paused. "Well, ex-wife, more accurately."

I gave him a curious look. "If you don't mind my asking, why were you going with your ex-wife to a work function?"

He took a long sip, considering.

"Life is messy," he said.

"Is that your mean law firm's slogan as well?"

"Could be," he said. "Could be. . . . But how about you? Have you ever been married?"

I nodded, as he looked down at my empty ring finger, which I felt the need to cover up. "And now separated. But that's not why I'm not wearing the ring. My nephew ate it."

He tilted his head. "I'm going to let that go," he said.

"Probably a wise move."

Then he gave me a smile—a very kind smile. "I'm sorry, though," he said. "It's hard. But it gets less hard."

"You sure about that?" I said.

"Very sure," he said. "Being in a city as great as London helps . . . being near cities as great as Dublin and Edinburgh and Rome help. The rosemary potatoes here *really* help."

As if on cue, my double order of rosemary potatoes arrived—piping hot and smelling a little like heaven.

I looked from the potatoes to him. "Did you plan that?"

"Afraid I don't have that kind of power," he said.

Then Aly—my new friend, apparently—reached for one of my potatoes. And looked back down at his paper, flipping to a new page.

"So you can eat in peace now," he said. "But I wanted to say hello first . . . and get you a decent drink . . . and steal a potato . . . and talk entirely too much, apparently, without even hearing you say your name. . . ."

"Annie," I finished for him.

"Annie."

He handed me his business card. "You can hang on to that if you like, for whenever you want a break from work, or a break from your typical breaks from work . . ." he said. "I'll take you potato hunting. No strings attached."

"Potato hunting?"

He pointed at my double order of rosemary goodness. "I assume you're a potato woman," he said.

I wasn't sure what kind of woman I was, but a potato one didn't seem like a bad place to start. Another evening as nice as this one was shaping up to be didn't seem like a bad place either.

So I looked down at his card.

It had the name of the place he worked—not a massive law firm, but rather . . . BECKETT MEDIA.

It also had his name, just sitting there: CALEB BECKETT.

I looked back up at him. "You're Caleb Beckett?"

"My friends call me Aly, remember?"

I held the card up, like proof. "But I'm not your friend," I said. "I'm your employee."

He shrugged. "Not a very immediate employee, you'd have to say, wouldn't you? Or we wouldn't just be meeting now," he said. "If you want to play it that way though, I'm going to have to advise you against wearing rhinestones to work."

I pulled the coat more tightly around me. "But why don't you have an Australian accent? Do you really have an ex-wife? And what kind of nickname is Aly? And why lie?"

He started counting down on his left hand, holding up all four fingers.

"I haven't had an accent since I was in my second year at Yale," he said. "And I only get to *wish* my ex-wife was part of a made-up tale. Aly is quite a common nickname for Caleb, where I come from. And I kind of thought that if I lied, I had a better chance of getting some potatoes."

Then he took another, and I slapped his hand away. "This gets worse and worse," I said.

"Not worse and worse," he said. "Better and better."

"How do you figure?"

"Now you get to go home happy that the guy you are finding yourself attracted to isn't some terrible lawyer utilizing his overpriced skill set to protect brutal corporations hurting the environment," he said. "But just someone you know from work. What's the big deal about that?"

"First of all, I am not attracted to you."

"No?" he said, smiling.

"No," I said. "And, second of all, if you keep talking to me, I'm going to tell everyone at work you read the *Guardian*."

He shrugged. "I'll get my own potatoes, then," he said. "Since you're intent on ignoring magic."

"Good."

"Good." He was smiling bigger.

He motioned for the waitress to bring him his own order, and turned back to his paper. And I turned back to mine, the two of us eating, side by side, like that, paper by paper.

And when I got home that night, I opened up my heart-shaped pocket to find the business card inside of it. On the back, Caleb had written *Aly,* and a phone number that didn't match the others.

Oh, and also the following: *You are attracted. 97%.*

35

For the first two years of "Checking Out," I had an epigraph that ran underneath my byline—a quote from Ernest Hemingway. A simple one-liner that read, "Never go on trips with anyone you do not love."

I thought it was a great quote about travel, but ultimately Peter removed it. Not because we were receiving many letters finding fault with the sentiment. (Most of the readers who wrote in commented on their own personal nightmare tales of traveling with someone they didn't know well enough.) But Peter didn't care about the horror stories. He thought traveling with someone you *didn't* love—traveling with someone who was a stranger, even—provided its own set of treasures. That it gave a trip a certain dramatic energy.

And he was right. But what Peter was missing was what I *loved* about what Hemingway wrote. It wasn't about the terrible stories, the miscommunications. Those happened, often during travel, with people who loved each other too. The bigger point for me was that if you were on a trip with someone you didn't love, at the end of it you'd only get to remember what you remembered. But if you went with someone you loved, you'd often get more than that. You'd get to share it with them. You'd get to remember what they remembered too.

The next day at work, almost as soon as I got to my desk, I heard a knock on the desk's high wall and looked up to see Melinda in that day's polka dots, which were a bright and friendly purple.

She gave me a big smile and before I could even say hello, she was sitting on the edge of my desk, her hand over her mouth.

"What?" I said.

"What, nothing?" she said. "Someone just made quite an impression on my cousin, that's all."

I looked down at my work, trying not to blush.

"He really is a good man," she said. "Despite my jokes about the subject. And he rarely takes a shine to anyone."

I rarely do too, I started to say. But the sentiment that came to my head on the heels of that, and far more loudly, was: *And I already know a good man. I already know a really great one.*

"Well, in any event, I'm sure it will pass," I said. "I often make a great impression when I'm not trying to."

"And then what happens?"

I shrugged. "I start to try and pretty much blow the whole thing up," I said.

She laughed. "Well, then," she said, "we better hurry and move forward with my excellent plan before that happens . . ." she said. "To a million first impressions!"

"I'm not following," I said.

"We have a plan. How to tell your one, big story," she said. "Ready for it? We are going to start *vlogging* you."

"That sounds dirty."

She patted my cheek, leaving her hand there. "Vlogging means we'll be filming you on each of your locations," she said. "A video column, if you will. And we're going to call it 'Checking In'!"

"'Checking *In*'?"

"Yes! It will explore the *one* thing that defines each city you visit. Plus, because it's only one thing you are focusing on, it will keep expenses down. Brilliant, no?"

She gave me an enormous smile, which, I guessed, was her way of answering her own question. Then she made a marquee sign with her hands. "Annie Adams: Europe's number one travel expert."

"Says who?"

"Says us!" she said. "It's part of Beckett Media's new synergy plan. This is the branding opportunity we were looking for. You'll be going on the local morning talk shows, news shows, et cetera. And eventually, when you are more comfortable, we'll go global. What do you think?"

"I think . . ." I looked right at her. "I'm a little confused. This will be in addition to writing 'Checking Out'?" I asked. "Like an in-depth video tour companion?"

"No no no. No companion. *In place of*," she said.

"In place of?" My eyes got wide. "I don't write anything anymore? There won't be a column?"

She clapped her hands together. "Exactly," she said. "And would you smile, please? What happens when I actually have to give you bad news one day? This is fabulous!"

"And I'm really grateful, Melinda, don't get me wrong . . ." I said, trying to figure out how to explain it. "But since we're talking about doing something new with the column, I actually had a different idea in mind."

She waved her hand in the air. "Well, have at it," she said. "I'm always open to ideas."

It was now or never, so I took a breath, trying to go for now.

"I've taken a lot of photographs during the years I've been working on 'Checking Out.' Pictures of people's homes, and I was thinking there was a story to tell around them? The way people live in different places. What that says about how we travel." I paused. "How we stay."

Melinda looked thoughtful for a minute, taking it in. "You know, I like it," she said. "I really like that."

"You do?"

She nodded. "I can picture you standing in front of a different home every month, vlogging with the people inside."

She really needed to stop saying "vlogging," but I was trying to focus on the positive. She liked the idea.

"You think there's something there?" I said.

"Absolutely," she said. "And this isn't an empty promise I'm making you. We will incorporate your vision into this. I *want* to do that."

I could tell that she meant it. I could tell that. And then, less than a minute later, I could tell she didn't care anymore. At least not in terms of where she felt that she needed to go next.

"But, the thing is, Annie, we have a great living and home expert. I need a travel expert. So let's keep that other idea on the back burner for now. And really enjoy this!"

Really enjoy this. All the signs were telling me to—to invest in my new life here, to move forward toward something entirely new. To move toward this bright new world waiting on the other side of my misshapen marriage, on the other side of a false start. This was the plan, wasn't it? To figure out how to be brave enough to find the life I wanted. To hold it, once it was found.

Melinda leaned in closer to me, jumping back in. And helping me to take it. The first step.

"So, in the interest of really enjoying this, you pick it," she said. "Anyplace in the world to do your first 'Checking In.' And I mean *any* place in the world. Where do you want to check in first? Where do you want to go most, Annie?"

Where do I want to go most in the world? The choices were piling up in my mind. Didn't I just hear an argument for Dublin and Edinburgh and Rome? Couldn't I make my own, solid argument for any of those places? For the hundreds of other places I was hoping to see?

Except what happened was, I couldn't. When Melinda actually presented the question to me, I couldn't make an argument at all. Or at least, not one I believed. Not when I knew there was one place I wanted to go. The one place I wanted to stay.

The one place I'd seen that felt different than the rest—right from the start. From the first time I drove down its sleepy Main Street, past the church steeple and the post office, all the Christmas trees still standing, light snow falling onto the remnants of a previous day's thick snowfall. And suddenly I knew why. Why I'd felt so content that day. It hadn't been about finding someplace new to explore, or escaping to a new life. It was about the person beside me. It was about what happened when we were together—what had been happening, for me, from the very start.

Which is when I stood up.

"Melinda, thank you so much for this opportunity," I said. "It is so generous, and I can't tell you how much it means to me."

She gave me her smile, beaming it right up at me.

"But I quit."

"*What?*" she said. I thought she was going to fall right out of her ballet slippers.

"I'm sorry," I said. "You deserve a better explanation than this, but I can't give it to you right now."

I started picking up my things as fast as I possibly could. Because that was the other thing. When you saw where the truth was, you wanted to get there as quickly as you could, before you lost sight of it again.

"Annie, do you know what you're giving up?" she said. "If we move forward, by this time next year you'll be a household name. Who wouldn't love that?"

Only the person who doesn't want this anymore, I thought. That person. That person was perhaps the only one who wouldn't see this as the next step forward. Toward wherever forward was.

"A crazy person, I would guess," I said. Then I shrugged, apologetically. " I have to go."

Five minutes later I was outside, running toward Regent Street—my phone to my ear—as I tried to make my way closer to the one person I had to tell: what I'd figured out, what I wanted most.

In the meantime, I was making a phone call. I was making a call that needed to be made. But I was relegated to voice mail. I was relegated to the voice mail of the one person I most needed to reach first.

"Hey Nick," I said, after the beep came on. "Can you give me a call when you get this? I need to talk to you. I think I should talk to you in person, probably, but either way I need to ask you something. . . ." I started to hang up. "Oh, and it's Annie, by the way."

Then I went to hail a cab—to get me to my flat, and then to Heathrow Airport, to fly to Logan Airport and get myself to western Massachusetts, exactly where I needed to go—but before I could, the phone rang.

The phone rang and the number I couldn't believe I was seeing right then—a number I was so happy to be seeing right then—came up, and then a voice I couldn't believe I was hearing was there, talking to me, too fast.

"Annie, you need to come here, okay?" he said. "You need to get on a plane and come home."

"What's going on?" I asked.

Then, as time stopped, Jesse told me.

36

If my life depended on it, I don't think I could tell you how I managed to get to the airport (I assume a taxicab), or onto the plane at Heathrow (I must have shown my passport, but did I have it with me? I don't recall having it with me), or how I got from Logan Airport in Boston to the emergency waiting room at Cooley Dickinson Hospital. I probably couldn't tell you, and wouldn't want to see a video of the evidence.

But somehow I ended up there, in the cold, badly lit emergency waiting room, looking around until I spotted Jesse slumped in the corner with a woman I'd never seen before. A woman I'd never seen before with bright red hair I had seen twice before—on Sammy and on Dexter. *Cheryl.*

They jumped up out of their chairs, out of their stupor, Jesse throwing his arms around me, seemingly relieved to have something to do, even if it was as useless as letting me know what was going on.

"It's called status asthmaticus," Jesse said.

My heart was pounding—I could actually feel how hard—now that I had stopped moving.

Cheryl turned toward Jesse. "Jess, don't scare her," she said. "Talking like that is going to scare her."

I almost folded right there, at such a small and necessary kindness.

"Basically," she said, keeping her voice soft and low, "it's a serious asthma attack."

"How serious?" I said.

"We don't know yet," Jesse said.

I looked down and away, as if not looking at Jesse would manage to make that part less true.

"His chest closed down," Jesse said. "He was out cold when someone found him, in the back of the kitchen."

"At the restaurant?"

Jesse nodded. "And the question is how long he was like that before we got to him," he said. "We don't know for how long. He's been working all the time, and he just forgot his inhaler. If he'd had it . . ."

"I get it," I said.

"He hasn't done that since he was a kid," he said.

"They've got him on a mechanical ventilator," Cheryl said. "And he has tubes and a mask on. You should know that too. Before you go in . . ."

Then she touched my arm gently, like we knew each other. And I guess, in a way, we did.

"Is that your way of telling me it looks worse than it is?"

"That's my way of telling you it still *is* worse than it is," she said. "The doctor said we almost lost him. We don't know the repercussions yet."

Lost him.

This was when I noticed her. Coming into the waiting room—coming back into the waiting room—holding a tray of insipid cafeteria food. And looking worried in the way only a mother could when her child was in danger.

Emily.

She drilled me with a look. She drilled me with such a look of consternation that when she remembered herself enough to give me a small smile, I knew that not only wasn't everything forgiven between us, maybe none of it was.

And still, she cleared her throat. "We'll be here when you come out," she said.

It was all I could do not to rush her right then, and collapse into the tears that I refused to let come.

"I appreciate that," I said. Then I turned back to Cheryl and Jesse. "Which way?"

Jesse pointed, and I went.

....

Griffin woke up slowly, and I moved from the chair where I had been sleeping to the side of the hospital bed.

He opened his eyes, trying to focus. Until he was looking at me, confused. "Hey," he said.

"Hey . . ."

I bent down—half kneeling, half standing—an awkward half position, so we were exactly at eye level.

"They called you?" he said.

"Yes," I said, talking low, matching his voice, trying not to look too hard at him. It felt like its own betrayal to look too hard, especially this close, at how he looked lying there. More than the tubes or the other tubes or the oxygen mask. More than the heartbeat of a machine, connected to him. His skin so pale, his green eyes weak and wrong. And I started to understand it then—what made Griffin, Griffin. That light coming off of him. What happened when it went missing.

He closed his eyes again. "I told them not to call you," he said.

I felt that in my chest, like a punch. I got it, of course. He didn't want this to be the reason I was back. He didn't want this to be how I decided anything. Was this the right time to tell him it wasn't? That I'd already decided? I didn't think so. Because it wasn't just about that. Maybe he'd already decided he wanted something else himself.

"Do I still get to get in?"

His nodded. "Sure."

I slipped into bed beside him, lying down, holding closely there, my face against his chest. Listening to his heart, which seemed slow to me. But what was my basis of comparison? Why hadn't I paid attention before, so I'd have one? This seemed, suddenly, like the most brutal thing of all.

"Do you remember what happened?" I asked.

"Some of it," he said. "Like . . . I do remember the best and the worst thing."

I looked up toward him, my chin still resting right there— resting on his chest again. "Really?" I said.

He nodded. "I went to the restaurant early Monday morning. A little before seven A.M. To try to do some inventory."

"So that's the worst?"

"That's the worst," he said.

"And what's the best?"

"I didn't have to do inventory."

I felt myself start to smile, turning so my cheek was resting against his chest. *Almost lost him.* Cheryl's words echoing in my head, loudly, making it hard not to turn the smile into tears. Right there. But I wasn't going to let that happen. I wasn't going to let myself cry.

"That is a good thing," I said.

"I definitely thought so."

Then, I could feel Griffin drifting—and I wrapped my arms around his chest, covering as much of him as I could.

"You look different," he said.

"No, I don't," I said.

"No," he said. "Not so much."

He paused, not saying anything for a minute. Neither of us saying anything.

"You'll be here when I wake up?" Griffin said, finally.

"I'll be here when you wake up," I said.

Then, as he started to fall back to sleep, he moved in closer to me, just a fraction, just until I felt his hand on the small of my back, holding us there.

I lay there next to my husband, listening to him breathe, as if my life depended on it. And, in the ways it mattered most, it did.

felt someone shake me awake a few hours later—was it a few hours later? I had no clue. All I knew was that Jesse was before me again, two enormous cups of coffee in his hands. My eyes went to the clock, which read 5:08. But was it A.M. or P.M.? I had no idea, the dark hospital room casinolike, only low light coming in through the closed shades.

"What's going on?" I asked.

"I have to show you something," Jesse said.

I blinked hard, still trying to acclimate, still trying to believe this was where I was, Griffin breathing softly and soundly— thankfully—beside me, beneath me.

I shook my head, adamant. "No," I said. "I told him I'd be here when he wakes up again."

"He's already woken up again," Jesse whispered. "You're way behind the times."

"I am?" I blinked a few more times. "Is it morning or night?" I asked.

Jesse reached out his hand for me to take. "Come and see," he said.

....

It was night. And ten minutes later, we were pulling out of the hospital parking lot and driving out into it, down Route 9 in Jesse's beat-up car, coffees in hand, the Avett Brothers singing to us from the radio.

I turned toward him, watching him tap on the steering wheel, to the music's slow beat.

"So," I said. "No chance you're going to tell me where we're headed?"

Jesse shrugged. "What, you new here or something?"

I shook my head, smiling. "I guess not," I said.

Then I turned back to face the road, and whatever was in front of us.

"You must have been surprised to see Cheryl in the waiting room earlier?" he said.

"I'm trying not to be surprised by anything these days," I said.

"Too risky?" he said.

"Exactly." Then, biting on my coffee cup's lid, I peeked at him out of the corner of my eye. "You feel like talking about it?" I asked.

"What's there to say, really?" Jesse shrugged. "We're having two more."

"Babies?"

"Twins." He smiled, shaking his head. "Yep, twins."

My jaw must have been on the floor, must have actually made it all the way down there.

"What is even the statistical probability of that?"

He stopped smiling, his eyes getting thoughtful as he considered.

"Well, actually . . ." he said, *"statistically,* once you have one set of twins, I believe you are twice as likely to have a second set in another pregnancy."

I looked at him in disbelief. "It's amazing, because you look like a normal person," I said.

"I know," he said. "You'd almost believe I was just offered the associate professor position in the Department of Physics and Applied Physics at UMass."

"UMass, here?"

He nodded. "UMass, right here."

I shook my head. "I mean, a girl goes away for a few weeks . . ." I said.

"It's amazing what the desire to provide for three more babies will do to your motivation level," he said. And he was smiling so big—so proud—that I almost didn't want to ask him about baby *three*.

"And Jude Flemming?"

"Jude Flemming is currently proud of me for being offered the associate professor position in the Department of Physics and Applied Physics at UMass," he said. "And we're going to work out the rest."

"Really? How?"

He turned and looked at me.

"Sorry, I didn't mean for it to come out like that."

"No, I get it. I have no idea . . ." He turned back to the road, and sighed. "The calm continueth not long without a storm," he said.

"You lost me there."

"The origin of the expression, the calm before the storm," he said. "From an unknown source in the sixteenth century. But it started a little different than how it's evolved. I like it more. The original idea that the calm can't last, not if you're really living. If you're living fully, the storm's coming to get you."

I gave him a look. "Now, you're showing off, Professor," I said.

"Someone has to," he said.

I started to laugh.

"It wasn't easy convincing her, though," he said. "To try again."

"Cheryl?" I asked. "How did you?"

He smiled sheepishly. "The pregnancy gave me the chance to finally sit down with her and tell her. That, in her absence, I figured out the secret."

"To what?"

He shrugged. "You know, *love*."

"Oh, that," I said.

"That," he said.

But before I could ask what he thought he had figured out, Jesse was pulling over to the side of the road and stopping the car. He was stopping the car behind a small building I knew very well. Griffin's restaurant.

"This is where we're going?"

"Yep," he said, turning off the ignition.

"Why?" I asked.

But I was pretty much talking to no one, because he was already out of the car, walking around to open my door for me.

"Follow me," he said, as I stepped outside.

And I did.

I followed him to the front of the restaurant, where I saw the large, red sign—the one matching the red door, the one previously resting beside it, nameless—now hung up, and ready for the world to see. No longer blank. A name on it. In lovely black, block letters. Just one word, just a one-word name:

HOME

I looked up at it, taking it in. "Home," I said. "I like it."

Jesse just nodded, giving me a small, unrecognizable smile. Then he unlocked the door and held it open for me.

I walked inside, and I was at a loss. How could I explain it? How could anyone begin to explain it? The moment where everything becomes unstuck: the world around you suddenly moving both slower and quicker, until you are completely and totally present in it. Your everything.

The empty walls of Griffin's restaurant were now full. They were completely full of the most beautiful frames you'd ever seen: black and metal and wood and mirrored frames.

My photographs inside each one.

All of my photographs, like nothing had happened to them. Like they didn't meet their demise among blueberries and little boys and barbeque sauce. Like they were here, like they'd always been right here. Exactly where they belonged.

I touched the wall in disbelief. A grand Flemish town house beside an even grander Nantucket Craftsman; a modern Cape Town flat next to a converted Prenzlauer Berg church.

"How did he do this?"

Jesse was standing right behind me, his hands folded in front of him. "It's amazing . . ." he said. "When you're willing to do the work, it's amazing what can be saved."

I was overwhelmed, though *overwhelmed* felt like too small a word to hold what I was feeling.

I turned toward him, tears filling my eyes, falling down my cheeks.

"So is that it? Is that the secret, or something?" I asked.

He tilted his head, looking at me. "What?"

"Is that your secret to *love?*"

"Oh!" He nodded, understanding. "No, but that would've been a good one too."

My tears turned to laughter as I reached out and hugged him, drying my eyes on my sleeve. I held my sleeve there, against my face, more tears spilling out. And from over my shoulder, I was looking at the walls again—my walls—taking in all I could see.

"Mine was simpler," he said.

"What's that?" I said.

"Sometimes," Jesse said. "We just pick right."

38

When we got back to the hospital, Gia was heading out of the revolving door. Gia and Emily, more accurately, were heading out the revolving door *together*—right toward us.

Jesse started to change direction, heading toward the side door.

"Where are you going? They see us!"

"Don't care," he said. "Not going to deal."

I grabbed his arm, talking in a fierce whisper. "Jesse! Don't leave me alone here," I said. "Haven't we done this already?"

He disentangled himself from me, squeezing my shoulder. "Sure," he said. "It's our thing."

Then, with barely a wave, Jesse moved toward the side door, but not before he leaned into me and whispered into my ear.

"Oh, by the way, Gia is the one who found Griffin," he said. "Just so you don't feel sideswiped."

"What did you say?" I asked.

But he was already gone, and Gia and Emily were in front of me. Emily and Gia, standing close to each other, standing seemingly united, in their matching black coats and cashmere sweater sets—and matching in that they each looked the exact opposite of me: my hand reaching up to touch my disheveled hair, to pull at my ripped sweatshirt.

I gave them a smile. "Hi . . ."

They gave me one back. "Griffin said you were back," Gia said. "Welcome back."

"Thank you." I looked right at her, trying to figure out what to say about her finding him, knowing none of the details. "And thank you," I said.

"For what?"

"Finding him."

She gave me another smile, this one more meaningful. "Thank yourself for coming back. He's doing better," she said. "He's looking more like himself."

"I'm glad to hear you think so," I said, feeling something loosen something inside of me, feeling it starting to let go.

Then I turned toward Emily. "And I just saw the restaurant," I said. "I just saw Home . . ."

I started to add that it looked incredible. But *incredible* felt tiny in comparison to how I felt about it. So I had to hope Emily heard it, in my silence.

Amazingly, Emily seemed to. "He did a wonderful thing there, didn't he?" she said.

"He did," I said.

And she nodded, further agreeing with herself. Which wasn't the same thing as complimenting—or even commenting on—my photographs now lining the walls. As commenting on why. But it wasn't *not* the same thing either. I chose to focus on that part.

"I should probably be heading home," Gia said. "Brian's been waiting for me."

Then Emily pushed Gia's hair behind her ear. "Okay, sweetie," she said. "Thanks again for checking in."

"Tell G I'm here if he needs anything."

"Of course," Emily said.

G? She called him G. No big deal. Just something I didn't know. She called him G, and she knew, maybe even better than I did, what it meant for him to look like himself. They had history—a lengthy, deep history—and that was never going away.

But now we had some history too, far more critical to deal with. Our first marriage. The first time through. When we were starting to figure out what it meant to get things right.

Life is messy, Aly had said in London. *The calm continueth not long without a storm*, Jesse had said just a few hours before.

Looking at my mother-in-law and the daughter-in-law she'd no doubt prefer—there was no denying that.

But still, we could let it be the other way too, couldn't we? At least some of the time? Especially when the most important thing was just almost lost for us.

Couldn't I—right now—let life be incredibly, incredibly . . . simple?

In the spirit of that, I gave them another smile, a fearless one. "It's really good to see you both."

Then I reached out and hugged them both to me, like it was the most natural thing in the world to do. It was a triangulated hug, with two sides of the triangle standing there as stiff as could be. Just waiting for it to be over.

Finally, Gia awkwardly pulled away.

Then Emily followed, straightening her skirt, trying unsuccessfully to hide her bafflement.

"Well," she said. "Okay, then."

I don't care. Still. It was so worth a shot.

. . . .

I watched Griffin sleep from my vantage point on his hospital room windowsill: his mask now off, the tubes starting to disappear.

He'd been sleeping for hours as I sat there, the sun coming up behind me. I watched him and tried to figure out how to do it. How to begin to say thank you for the restaurant. How do you thank someone for having that kind of sure-hearted belief in you, that kind of faith in your future? At the very least, by being honest, I decided.

Which was when Griffin woke up.

He turned toward me, covering his eyes with his arm, at first, to block out the little bit of sun coming in toward him. Then, adjusting to it, he put his arm behind his head. And gave me his smile.

"Hi there," he said.

"Hi there," I said. "How are you feeling?"

He felt around for it, the real answer.

"I'm feeling a little better, I think . . ." he said. "Somewhere between a little better, and a lot."

And he looked it. Gia had been right about that. He wasn't there entirely, not just yet. But I could see the seeds, just below the surface. Pushing their way out.

"Good," I said. "And maybe this will help. The doctors are saying you can go home."

"Today?"

"Not today, but soon," I said. "Maybe tomorrow."

"I'll take soon. . . ." He nodded. "I'll take tomorrow. Maybe."

I gave him a smile and got off the windowsill, moving to the edge of the bed, dragging the hospital room's one chair with me. Straddling it, the high part between us.

He reached out and took my hand, held on to my fingers, between the chair's beams.

"Tell me something . . ." he said.

"What?"

"I want to know about London."

I looked down, looking at our hands, as if they had the answer. "I'm not sure where to start," I said.

"The beginning is usually a good bet," he said.

I nodded. "Well . . ." I said. "When your brother called me, to tell me what was going on with you, that you were in here, I had just quit my job. . . ."

Griffin gave me a confused look. "So how's that the beginning, exactly?" he asked.

I smiled. "I was leaving London anyway," I said. "I was leaving before all of this."

"Why was that?" he asked.

"It was a dream job," I said, giving him a small shrug. "But it turns out that you were right. It was someone else's dream."

Griffin nodded. But he stayed quiet, watching me, and waiting for the rest of it—waiting to hear where I was planning to go.

"But, the thing is, when your brother called, I was actually calling Nick to tell him that," I said. I took a deep breath, and shored myself up to say the rest of it. "When your brother called, that's what I was doing. I figured out what I wanted, and I was calling Nick to tell him."

"Tell him?" Griffin said.

"Maybe I should go back to the beginning. . . ."

Griffin squeezed my hand, laughing a little. "Now," he said. "Now she wants to go back to the beginning."

"I had to go to London, Griffin. Because I didn't know it before then," I said. "I didn't know the whole story yet."

"Which is what?" he said.

"Why I picked you."

I paused, meeting his eyes, so he could feel it. That I meant it, exactly what was coming.

"It wasn't on a whim. My whole life I've been searching for things that felt good enough. Looking out there, as far out there as I could get, for what might make me happy. I even managed to make a career out it. But then I found you. And you were only interested in *me* feeling good enough for me." I paused, trying to fight the tears in my eyes. "And you made me a restaurant so I would."

Griffin gave me a smile, and then he tried unsuccessfully to pull me toward him, through the chair. "I think you should come here," he said.

I nodded, and got into bed beside him, lying down on my side, the two of us facing each other, like that.

He kissed me on the forehead, then on both cheeks. "So . . ." Griffin said. "What about Nick, then?"

I tried to figure out how to say it, what I had figured out about Nick—what had taken me five years, a brutal breakup, and a belated marriage proposal to figure out: we loved each other. (I can be a slow learner, I know.) We loved each other in the difficult, unusable way where you took turns doing it, instead of ever managing to do it at the same time. You can't always do it at the same time, but you have to be able to sometimes. Because, ultimately, wasn't being good at it, together, the most important part?

And more than that, there was this. On the other side of Nick, I had *shifted*. Griffin had shifted me. That was what love could do, after all. And I didn't want to shift back to where I accepted less than what was at stake for me, right here, with Griffin. A place where I had to show up. Where I was learning how to let someone show up for me.

Griffin tilted his head toward me. "I'm just asking," he said, "if you realized all this in London, why did you call him?"

"Oh," I said, and nodded, vigorously, getting his question. "Because I realized something else too."

"What's that?" Griffin said.

"I want my dog back," I said.

I felt it against my chest, Griffin starting to smile, moving in to kiss me like that, smile still going. We kissed for a minute. And then he started to laugh.

"What's so funny?" I said, but then I was laughing too—just

at the sound of hearing his laugh—both of us laughing hard, I was a little afraid it might hurt him.

"I was hoping to get her before I got on the plane to come to you," I said. "But that didn't exactly work out."

"It's not that," he said, shaking his head. "That's really not what I was laughing about."

"What, then?"

"Jesse and I were looking out the window earlier," he said. "When you were talking to my mother and Gia."

My eyes got wide, understanding. "You saw the hug?" I said.

"I saw the hug, I even got it on film," he said.

I closed my eyes. "I'm mortified," I said.

"Don't be," he said. "I think in that moment you may have single-handedly brought me back to health."

"That's not nice," I said, blushing. But I relaxed into him anyway. For the first time, since we'd been so far away from each other, I felt myself truly relaxing.

"But Griffin?" I said, softer now, closer now. "I've been thinking about something else," I said.

"One more thing?" he said.

I nodded. "One more thing."

He looked right at me, pulling the hair off of my face. "Hit me," he said.

I leaned into his hand, which was still holding my hair. "I know it's silly, but I want a wedding. I want to buy a big, poufy white dress that costs too much, and to wear my tango shoes, and have a first dance in the backyard. I want to take a really awkward photograph with our mothers, and to get a really bad hangover the next day," I said. "I want to say this counts."

He got quiet for a minute, looking at me. Then he nodded. "I'm up for that."

"Good," I said. "I mean, it doesn't have to be tomorrow. But just, one day."

"Yeah," he said, "I'd say tomorrow is probably out."

I laughed, Griffin leaning into me, his mouth right by my ear.

"But so you know," he said, "if you say it softly right now, it will."

It took me a minute. It took me a minute to understand what he was saying. And it took me one last minute before I did it. "It counts," I said.

Then, as if on cue, the nurse came in, and told us we could go home.

39

M aybe the most important thing I learned from writing "Checking Out" was that there was no such thing as the perfect destination. To a certain degree, I understood that going in, but it became more clear to me every time that a reader asked the magic question: *If you could only take one more trip, where would you go?*

On any given day, I could choose Sicily, just to revisit the loveliest waterfall I'd ever seen; or Caracas, Venezuela, for the tiny staircase leading down to the greatest tango room I'll probably ever have the privilege of dancing in; or Brattleboro, Vermont, and that tiny bar that I'd happily spend half my life in, and not only because it has the best macaroni and cheese I ever tasted. Or that foresty inn in Big Sur, California, where my soul feels a little bit like it can take a breath without asking anyone's permission.

In the end—even if no one wants it be so complex (or so simple)—every place offers its own special treasures. But no place offers all of them. Which no one wants to hear. Because it puts it ultimately in our hands, doesn't it? What we choose to live with, and what we choose to live without.

Twenty-four hours before my thirty-third birthday—a few weeks after I was back in Williamsburg for good—I was sitting on the living room couch, trying to get some work done.

I was trying to get some work done as opposed to what I was actually doing, which was watching the Tee Ball game that wasn't exactly happening right outside of the bay window. The twins were in the backyard, running around the tee, playing some sort of impromptu game of tag, while a very excited Mila jumped up and down with the ball in her mouth.

I laughed, making myself look back at my computer screen. That was the deal, after all. I couldn't go outside until I was finished working on the introduction to my book. My *book*. It made me feel good to say it. (Good and a little bit terrified, though I was trying not to focus on that part.) It was a book of photography. It was centered around the photographs I'd taken of the beautiful homes. And centered around how one travel writer's journey ended when she found hers. Or, maybe, how it began again. However you wanted to look at it.

"Knock . . . knock."

I turned to find Griffin standing in the living room doorway, a ridiculously big bowl of buttered popcorn in his hands.

"Just wanted to see how it's going?" he asked.

"Well, if I can get you to bring that popcorn over here, I'm far more likely to tell you," I said.

He handed over the popcorn, taking a perch on the side of the couch. "So?" he said.

"Well, so far . . ." I looked down at my computer screen, then back up at him. "I've written fifteen of the introduction."

His eyes got wide. "Pages?"

"*Words.*"

Griffin got quiet, considering this. "Are they good ones?"

"They aren't bad," I said.

"You sound like you deserve a break," he said.

"Oh, thank goodness!"

I closed the laptop, and reached for him, pulling him toward me for a long kiss. He held me there, against him, which allowed me to move me into the nook, right into the curve in his chest. The truth was, I was still doing it, listening to his heartbeat like that, far too often. I imagined there would come a time when I wouldn't. Or it wouldn't scare me in the same way. But, for now, it did.

Griffin kissed the top of my head. "So I was thinking," he said, "since tonight's my night off, we could watch a movie, if you want."

"Sounds good," I said.

"Yeah?"

I took a large handful of popcorn. "Definitely," I said. "What did you have in mind?"

As an answer, Griffin clicked on the DVD player, a movie already in there sneakily ready to go, the opening sequence coming to life on the screen: the crisp white credits, that fabulous orchestra, the Vatican coming across the screen. *Roman Holiday.*

I pointed at the television, the popcorn spilling from my open fist, onto the floor. "No!!!" I said.

"*Yes.*"

I didn't even bother dusting off my hands before putting them over my eyes. Fast as I could.

"Have you lost your freaking mind? What are you doing to me?" I said, my voice rising to a surprisingly high volume. "I can't see anything! Whoever is listening, whoever decides these things, I didn't see anything worth mentioning. I didn't see anything, barely *at all,* that should bring on the bad."

I was yelling toward the ceiling at this point—it's sadly true—but Griffin was laughing too hard to hear just how loud. (He did hit PAUSE first, bless his heart.) He was laughing and gently removing my hands from over my eyes, kissing each of them, holding them in his lap.

"You trust me, right?" he said.

I looked at him, his sweet face. His knock-you-out smile—*this* close to being too smooth for its own good.

"Very much," I said.

"Then trust me that it'll be fine. I promise you."

"You don't get it. You can't promise that." I pointed at the screen again. "You turn that on, and I may as well just sit here and wait for the bad to happen."

He shrugged. "Well, I guess I have a different idea."

"What? You think you can turn it all around? Make *Roman Holiday* bring some good luck after all this time?"

"More like, I think the bad is probably coming anyway, so you may as well enjoy the movie."

"That's depressing!"

"That's life," he said. "It's a great movie. It'd be good to enjoy it."

It would. It would be good to enjoy it. For all the reasons it was my favorite movie—and one more reason that, maybe, was only occurring to me now. For a moment there, Audrey found it. Amidst the crazy experiment of taking a day to live life on her own terms. She did find it. The place she felt like she belonged.

"Here we go . . ." Griffin said.

Then he clicked PAUSE again, and turned the volume up higher, the movie coming to life on the screen.

"And I'll be here for you," he said. "If and when the bad does come. For whatever it's worth."

It was worth a lot. How could I tell him how much? I would spend my life trying.

And, still, I picked up my computer and hauled ass out of that room, as fast as my legs would carry me.

ater that night I found myself once again in front of my computer—my house quiet, dark, happy—Mila sleeping by my feet, her weight keeping them warm. I was writing an e-mail to Jordan.

The subject line read: MY FINAL "CHECKING OUT" COLUMN. And this is what the e-mail said:

CHECKING OUT

by Annie Adams

WHY I'M LIVING WITH CHEF BOYARDEE IN THE MIDDLE OF NOWHERE

Open Your Eyes:
And look at his.

Leave Your Comfort Zone:
To quote Peter's good friend John Steinbeck: "I've lived in good climate, and it bores the hell out of me. I like weather rather than climate." Here's hoping, one of these days, I agree with Steinbeck.

Find the Special Sauce:
I recommend the lobster and eggs, preferably in the middle of the night, sitting on a cold kitchen counter. There's nothing better than waiting for that next bite, which (even if it shouldn't be possible) is always better than the last.

Take the Wrong Exit:
Some might say western Massachusetts is a wrong exit. Especially after the "perfect" exit: one leading to a place to call my own on the best block in London, to a high-flying career, to a second basil martini, to a new life that could be anything. But here's the thing that I've learned about this open-ended daring, the thrill associated with endless escape: it gets less thrilling. Especially once you've found the courage to choose something you don't really want to escape from.

Discover the One Thing You Can't Find Anywhere Else:
I told Griffin about *Roman Holiday*. He's the first person I've told since you. And he tried to make me sit down and watch it with him. So I would understand we were in it together. All of it. The good, the bad, the ridiculous. And like that, I feel safe in all three. . . . So don't worry. We are taking it slow, and he *is* married. But it turns out he's married to me, so I'm thinking we may have a good shot.

I started to shut the computer down for the night—to go upstairs and get into bed with Griffin, to leave whatever else was coming until tomorrow—but Jordan wrote me back, almost immediately.

To The Editor:

I will admit that I enjoyed this column. Especially the last part. I shouldn't have to carry all the information regarding Annie's *crazy* alone. Glad I won't have to anymore.

Please tell her not to get too excited*,* but we're thinking about coming for a visit. Okay*,* we're definitely coming. She can be as excited as she likes.

We can't wait. Apparently*, the middle of nowhere* is the most beautiful place in the world when the leaves start to turn.

Acknowledgments

I would like to thank my family and friends, who were tremendously supportive while I worked on this book.

Thank you to the fantastic team at Viking Penguin, who has made a home for me for three books now. I am grateful to everyone there, especially my wonderfully insightful editor Molly Barton. For their wisdom and expertise, a special thank you to Clare Ferraro, Nancy Sheppard, Shannon Twomey, Andrew Duncan, Maureen Donnelly, and Stephen Morrison.

Thank you to my dynamite and very wise agents—Gail Hochman and Sylvie Rabineau—for their invaluable guidance.

Thank you to my early readers for helping in many ways: Allison Winn Scotch, Jonathan Tropper, Dustin Thomason, Heather Thomason, Ben Tishler, Dahvi Waller, Camrin Agin, Michael Fisher, Jessica Bohrer, Amy Cooper, Sam Baum, Jonas Agin, Bonnie Carrabba, Liz Squadron, Brett Forman, Melissa Rice, Alisa Mall, Carolyn Earthy, Becca Richards, Paula and Peter Noah, Gary Belsky, Brendan and Amanda O'Brien, Andrew and Crystal Li Cohen, Debora Cahn, Michael Heller, Shauna Seliy, and Dana Forman, who read this book too many times to count.

Many thanks to the wonderful book clubs and bookstores that have made me feel so welcome with their enthusiasm and warmth.

For their love and support, thank you to my brother Jeff, and to the entire Dave and Singer families.

A special thank you to my mom and my dad—Rochelle and Andrew Dave—who raised me to love books and writing. I am so grateful to be their daughter.

Finally, my gratitude and love to Josh Singer, my favorite writer, who not only cared for every page of this book as much as I did, but who sang to me from *The Gleam* whenever I requested. And who is my favorite part of every day.